DISTANT
LAUGHTER

Anthea Holland

Published in 2010 by New Generation Publishing

CHAPTER ONE

"Come on, Sue, we'll be late for tea." Nita waited impatiently for her friend, tapping her foot as she watched Sue negotiate the steep bank. Nita held out her hand and yanked Sue up the last few feet.

"What's the hurry?" panted Sue; "You're not usually this worried about getting home in time for meals"

"Eric's coming to tea and Mum threatened me if I was late I'd have to go without."

"Ah." Sue's nod said she understood and the two girls made their way along the lane towards the cottages at the crossroads where they parted, Sue to head back to the village and Nita to face her mother's wrath.

"Where have you been?" Maureen demanded of her daughter, "I told you four o'clock and just look at you. Five minutes before Eric's due to arrive, and you're still thick with mud. Be off to the bathroom with you this minute and I want you back here, clean and scrubbed, in five minutes flat."

"I don't know what all the fuss is about, it's not me he's coming to see."

"Don't be cheeky, girl, or you'll feel the back of my hand on your behind."

Nita felt the tension in the air and scurried up the narrow stairs to the room she shared with her sister, Scarlett. Collecting the clean clothes her mother had already laid out on the bed, she bounded down the stairs two at a time and made her way through the kitchen to the bathroom at the rear of the house. Nita's parents were very proud of their bathroom, a recent edition to the building. The only drawback was that anyone in the kitchen saw the comings and goings.

Scarlett was busy at the kitchen sink.

"Good grief, Nita, aren't you ready yet?"

"Don't flap, I won't be long." Nita disappeared into the bathroom, emerging seven minutes later in a pretty pink dress with white bow belt. This time her father was in the kitchen.

"My, my, don't you look pretty," he grinned at his daughter, knowing just how she must be feeling.

"Oh, Dad! I look awful, and I'm going to be scared to do anything in case I get dirty."

"You'll do, don't you worry." Her father put a reassuring arm round her "And you really do look as pretty as a picture. Give it a few years and you'll be breaking all the hearts in West Morling."

Nita snorted. "I don't want to break any hearts. I can't be bothered with boys, they're all stupid."

"What about David and Leo, you spend enough time with them?"

"That's different, they're friends. They don't go all moony eyed when they see me or strut around trying to look clever."

"We'll see. Well, you'd best go and put in an appearance, Eric's been here a good five minutes."

"Ah, he'll not notice me anyway, all he's got eyes for is our Scarlett, they make a good pair those two."

"Now, now, that's enough of that, let's not make fun of your sister."

"Sorry, Dad," Nita gave him a rueful smile as she left the poky kitchen and made her way through to the front room. Her mother liked to call it the parlour but none of the rest of the family ever called it anything but the front room. The furniture in it was old but unworn, the dark oak almost unmarked by use. Each afternoon Maureen drew the curtains to stop the sun from fading the wood and consequently the curtains, once a rich emerald green, were now almost cream, but the three piece suite still retained it's original golden hue.

Eric was perched uncomfortably on the edge of the armchair, a cup of tea held rigidly in his hands, his earnest eyes in his plain face gazing adoringly at Scarlett through pebble glasses.

Scarlett, meanwhile, sitting in the other armchair, was wearing what Nita called her 'soppy' expression as she gazed back at Eric. Her hair, which Scarlett liked to describe as auburn but which was, in fact, ginger, was scraped back in an unbecoming fashion and tied with an elastic band.

God knows what they see in each other, Nita thought, as she sat beside her mother on the settee.

"Dad won't be a minute." Maureen smiled apologetically at Eric, "He's just going to wash his hands, then he'll be through and we can start tea."

Eric dragged his eyes away from Scarlett and looked at his hostess. Nita thought that for a moment he had trouble remembering what he was there for before his gaze cleared.

"No hurry, Mrs. Evans, no hurry." He looked at the spread on the trolley. "You've certainly gone to a lot of trouble, it all looks very appetising."

"It's no trouble at all, Eric."

Mr. Evans' entrance into the room hid Nita's snort of derision at her mother's words. 'No trouble,' indeed! Hadn't her Mother slaved over a hot stove for the past two days to prepare the cakes and flans now resplendent on the tea trolley? And all because soppy Eric Williams liked Scarlett and Mum fancied Eric as a son-in-law because he was an accountant and, compared to the Evans, rather well off.

Dan grinned at Nita as he took the seat next to her before turning his attention to his older daughter and her suitor. "Well, I'm here, let's make a start."

Scarlett got up and poured the tea out and handed it round while Maureen distributed the sandwiches. Dan stayed in his chair and was waited on because that was the way it always was and Nita made no attempt to help because she and the family knew from experience that if she did it would likely end in disaster.

After tea Nita was excused and thankfully went and changed back into her old skirt and jumper, hanging the dress carefully on a hanger as she'd been taught. She was dismayed to see a smear of jam down the front of it, but relieved to find she hadn't ripped it anywhere.

It was too dark to play out of doors at this time of year and Jenny and David, who lived next door, were staying with their Aunt in Suffolk, so it looked like another boring evening on her own. If she could have gone home with Sue she could have had tea at the Big House with Sue and her mum and dad and Sue's Dad would have run her home. Instead she had the choice of an early night (yeuk!) or sitting in the living room with Mum and Dad. It was too dark to play in the loft, where Dad had made a play-room for her, as there was no electric light and she'd been forbidden to use the oil lamps.

In the end she decided to go downstairs. Maybe Mum and Dad would have a game of cards with her or something, but then she remembered the dreaded Eric. Would he still be there or not? She crept quietly down the stairs, avoiding the fifth stair that she knew, from her occasional forays to the pantry for a midnight feast, creaked. The lights were on in the kitchen and she crept to the door. Her mother was at the sink, washing up, while her father was cleaning the family's shoes.

"I don't know if we should have let them go off together like that," her Mother said.

"Now stop your worrying, woman. Eric's a sensible lad and Scarlett's been brought up properly hasn't she? For goodness sake, they've only gone for a walk up to the old farm and they're so bundled up with clothes that I don't think they'll be inclined to get up to anything." He closed the lid on the shoebox and slid it into place under the sink. Standing up, he put his arm round Maureen"' shoulders and kissed her on the cheek. "Mind you, what's wrong for them could be good for us."

"Hush now, Dan. Can't you think of anything else?"

"Not with a beautiful woman like you around, no."

Maureen smiled at her husband, and their eyes locked in unspoken communion. Nita didn't know what they were going on about but she sensed they wouldn't want her overhearing. She crept back up the stairs and then bounded down them, confident that this time they would hear her. Sure enough, her father was sitting at the table when she entered and her mother was busily wiping up and putting away the tea things.

"So where's Sis and her lovely boyfriend, then?" questioned Nita as she took a seat at the table opposite Dan.

"They've gone for a walk," Maureen replied, "And that's enough sarcasm from you, young lady. Eric's a very nice young man, just the sort of husband I would wish for my daughter."

Nita kept silent, but groaned inwardly. She hoped to goodness that her mother's tastes had mellowed by the time it came to her turn to choose a husband.

Maureen picked up a pile of ironing and Nita heard her climbing the stairs to the bedrooms to put it away. Dan put his hand on Nita's slender arm where it lay on the table.

"Don't mind her, lass," he said as though he could read her mind, "She only wants what's best for both of our fine daughters. Anyway, you don't want to discourage Eric do you?"

"Don't I?"

"For sure you don't. Once Scarlett gets married, won't you have a whole bedroom to yourself?"

Nita was stunned. It simply hadn't occurred to her that the romance might benefit her in any way.

"I hadn't thought," she said at last.

"No, I didn't think you had. Well, that's given you something to think about now, hasn't it?"

Nita pictured the bedroom without all Scarlett's bits and pieces in it. Why, the top of the dressing table would be empty without all those jars and bottles, and wouldn't it be Heaven to have all the bed to herself? Suddenly a thought struck her.

"Dad, can I have a dog?"

The smile faded from Dan's face. "No, of course you can't. You've been told time and time again - no dog."

"But you always said we hadn't got room, and when Scarlett goes there'll be lots of extra space."

"We'll see. There's a lot more to having a dog than just the room for it to sleep. It needs plenty of exercise and someone to feed it."

"I'll do it," Nita said eagerly.

"We'll see," Dan said again, "There's plenty of time, Eric hasn't even asked me if he can marry Scarlett yet."

"Can we have a game of cards or something, Dad?" Nita asked, pushing the thought of her own pet to one side for the time being.

"Wait till your Mother comes down and we'll see. Mind you, she's been very busy today and she might not feel like it," he warned.

When she came down, Maureen was only too pleased to take the weight off her feet and do something relaxing. Not that doing anything with her younger daughter could ever be relaxing, she decided. Nita had the voice of a foghorn and the energy of a lamb in spring. It fair wore her out just to watch her sometimes. Still, she was a good girl, seldom gave any trouble. Not like Shirley, Hannah's daughter. Hannah ran the village shop where Maureen sometimes worked, and she'd seen and heard the way Shirley behaved. Always answering Hannah back, she was, and constantly disobedient. At least Nita did what she was told. Most of the time, anyway.

"Your go, Mum." Nita's voice reminded her that her attention should be on the game of rummy that was currently taking place. She took her card from the pile. Ace of spades, just what she needed.

"Gin," she said, triumphantly laying her cards on the table.

"Oh, Mum, you've won again." Nita complained good-naturedly.

"Another game?" Maureen invited.

"Best not," Dan said, "That sounds like the youngsters coming home."

"I'm off to bed then." Nita jumped up off of her chair and kissed Dan goodnight. "Will you come up and tuck me in, Mum?" she asked, still unwilling to let go of the childhood ritual.

"I'll be up in a little while," Maureen promised, "Just let me make coffee for Scarlett and Eric...or maybe they'd prefer hot chocolate as it's so cold outside." She was still musing to herself as Nita climbed the stairs to the bedroom.

Eric and Scarlett came into the kitchen stamping their feet. They unwound the scarves from their necks and both opted for hot chocolate to drink. Scarlett took the outdoor clothes through to the hall where she hung them on the hooks under the stairs. She came back to the kitchen where Maureen had placed two steaming cups of chocolate on the table.

"There. That should warm you both up." She looked at their red cheeks and at her daughter's sparkling eyes and thought how nice it was to be young and in love.

Dan had buried his head in the local paper and Maureen sighed. She knew Dan wasn't keen on Eric, but he could at least make the effort to be polite for Scarlett's sake. Fortunately, Eric had eyes only for Scarlett and didn't seem to notice anyone else.

"She could do a lot worse," she told Dan later that night as they were preparing for bed.

"Happen she could, but I reckon she could do a lot better as well. That Eric's as wet as a long weekend, and about as exciting I shouldn't wonder." He caught sight of Maureen's expression and relented. "All right, all right. I'll try and do better next time. Promise."

Maureen rewarded him with a smile as she held his gaze for a moment before returning her attention to her face in the mirror. He knew it was important to her that her daughters made good marriages and was glad that it would be a few years before Nita was of marriageable age. Secretly, he thought Maureen would not find Nita as pliable as Scarlett. Their younger daughter tended to have a mind of her own and it seldom held the same views as her mother.

Dan knew that parents were not supposed to have favourites, just as he knew that Scarlett was Maureen's, but he couldn't help having a special place in his heart for his younger child. She looked very much the way Maureen had at the same age. Black curly hair and eyes nearly as dark that could melt a grown man's soul, but where Maureen had always looked demure and tidy, Nita somehow never managed to. Not that she tried very often. Dan was confident that she would one day grow out of the tomboy stage and turn into the beautiful, graceful woman that her mother had become.

He looked at Maureen now, as she approached their bed in a haze of shimmering white night-gown and thought how lucky he was. He knew from his drinking friends how most of their wives went to the marital bed with hair in rollers and muck on their faces and socks on their feet. Not to mention the winceyette pyjamas. Dan groaned. No, definitely best not to mention the winceyette pyjamas. Then he groaned again but for a different reason, as Maureen ran her hand across his stomach. He turned to face her and then she was in his arms and he forgot about other men's wives and his own errant daughters and concentrated only on the pleasure that was his.

***

It was the month before Christmas and Maureen was working in the village store every evening. There was no W.I. or choir practice for Hannah that month, nor drinks with the lads for her husband, Joe. All hands were needed to help cope with the extra demand the forth-coming festivities demanded.

Maureen and Joe were busy serving while Hannah prepared and packed the orders ready for delivery the following day. During a welcome lull between customers Maureen went through to the kitchen and put the kettle on to boil.

"Have you heard about the Big House?" Hannah asked.

The Big House was, in fact named "Church View", so called because it stood in the lane leading to the church. Everyone referred to it as "the Big House" though, despite it being only about half the size of Hill House, the house on the hill that stood overlooking the village.

"No, what's happened?"

"The Davidsons are moving. Mrs. D. was in here earlier. Apparently he's got a transfer with the bank and they're moving to somewhere in the Midlands." Her voice dropped to a conspiratorial whisper, "Between you and me, I don't believe he could afford to run that mausoleum."

Maureen thought that Hannah probably had a point. Richard Davidson had inherited the house on his mother's death five years before, but Maureen had always had the impression that there hadn't been much money with it.

"I was thinking of Nita, how she'll miss Sue," she commented.

"I hadn't thought of that, they're thick as thieves those two, aren't they?"

The ring of the shop bell brought their gossip to an end and Maureen went back to her place behind the counter. She couldn't help but feel sorry for Nita. She and Sue Davidson had been best friends since before they started school and it would be hard for them to have to part. When she got home that night Maureen decided not to say anything about the Big House to Nita deciding that it would be best if the news came direct from Sue.

**

In her cottage at the other end of the village Daphne Taylor lay sleepless, thinking of the news that had filtered through to her today. Daphne didn't have any friends in the village but Hannah Hughes, who ran the village stores, ignored Daphne's reticence, and always chatted away nineteen to the dozen. Daphne was convinced this was only good customer relationship and not really a desire to be friends. Still, it had been Hannah Hughes that had given Daphne the good news about the Davidsons.

Daphne recalled her lunch with Richard Davidson the previous week with some horror. It had been the culmination of seemingly unending calls and invitations from Richard, which she had constantly turned down. She had always been firm but polite, knowing that Richard, in his position at the bank, was the only person in West Morling who might have guessed the truth ... that somewhere in the world Daphne had a husband - well, an *ex*-husband really; an ex-husband who regularly paid money into her account so that she and Leo could survive.

For a long while Daphne hadn't been sure that Richard knew her secret, although working in the bank she guessed he could have ferreted it out, but he had never mentioned it ... until a week ago.

"I think it would be in your own best interests to join me," he had said after she had refused his latest invitation to lunch with him the following day. She had been in town, hurrying down the High Street in an effort to get all her shopping done before the eleven o'clock bus left, and she wondered if he had been standing by the window in the bank all morning in case she passed.

"I don't think so, Richard -" she began, but he interrupted her.

"Perhaps we could discuss Derek Taylor. He is your husband, I believe?"

Richard looked at her, and she knew her mouth was open and she looked ridiculous, but before she could reply he was off. "I'll see you at one, in Tamlins, the table right at the back," he called over his shoulder before disappearing through the heavy bank doors.

She shut her mouth and tried to pull herself together, but she was unable to concentrate on her shopping and, when she got home, found she had forgotten to get any vegetables at all.

"Well, I guess that doesn't matter, I'll get them tomorrow," she told Leo, knowing already that she would have to keep the lunch date with Richard.

The next day was dull and overcast. Fitting, Daphne thought, for someone who was going to their doom.

As she walked into Tamlins she felt as though all eyes were on her and wished she had worn a disguise. It wouldn't do for her to be seen having lunch with another woman's husband. Still, too late for that now.

Pulling her shoulders back and standing as tall as she could, she pretended a confidence she did not feel as she walked through to the back of the restaurant, to the table where Richard was waiting.

The food was wasted on her, all she could taste was the bile that rose in her throat as she listened to this obnoxious man who could destroy the years of lies that Daphne had carefully fabricated for herself.

"So, you see," said Richard as he pushed his own empty plate away and helped himself to a potato from her untouched meal, "I know you are not the widow Taylor that you claim to be. Personally, I can't see that it matters whether you have a husband or not, but it's obviously important to you, otherwise you would never have lied about it. So, what I propose .... "he leant forward and gazed into her eyes, and she could see the acne scars on his face and the hairs protruding from his nose, "to prevent me accidentally letting slip the fact that you are a married woman, you and I ... get it together, if you see what I mean."

Daphne did see what he meant. All too clearly. She watched his chubby little hands as they clutched the fork awkwardly as he chased a sprout round his plate. Suddenly she had an absurd desire to laugh. This pathetic little man thought he could blackmail her into sleeping with him. Because she was small and slight, men thought she was weak as well. They forgot she had years of living on her own behind her, of fighting for herself and her son and their rights.

She leaned forward herself so that her eyes were only inches away from the weak watery eyes of Richard Davidson. He drew back startled.

"Yes," she said, "I see what you mean. Quite an interesting idea, isn't it?"

She watched the look of puzzlement on Richard's face. This lunch was obviously not going the way he planned.

"Okay," she said. "I'll make a deal with you. You tell anyone, and I mean anyone, that I have a husband, and I'll tell your wife what you've just proposed." She held up a hand to prevent him speaking before continuing, "Plus," she said, "I will write to the bank and tell them. I'm sure they would be interested not only to learn that you have made unsavoury suggestions to one of their customers, but also to learn that you are prepared to reveal confidential information that you have uncovered from your duties at the bank."

She rose from her seat.

"I wish I could say 'thank you' for the lunch, but I didn't find it very pleasant. However, since you obviously enjoyed it, you may as well finish mine." She lifted her plate and tipped the remainder of the vegetables and meat pie, together with several spoonfuls of gravy into his lap, before replacing the plate firmly on the table and leaving the restaurant, her head held high.

In her single bed, Daphne breathed a sigh of relief. She had waited for repercussions. It was a fine line she had walked, but she had heard nothing since that day, and it looked as though she may have got away with it.

Snuggling under the covers, she fell into a deep, dreamless sleep, confident of her ability to continue to protect herself and her son.

CHAPTER TWO

It was a month after the tea party before Eric asked Dan if he could marry Scarlett. A month in which it seemed to Nita that Eric was at their house nearly all the time, except for the one weekend when he and Scarlett went to London to shop and see a show. They stayed with Eric's grandmother overnight in Romford rather than make the long journey home.

"Ahhh - bliss" thought Nita that night as she spread herself out beneath the blankets on the big double bed. "No big sister taking up all the room."

"Ahhh - bliss," thought Scarlett, as she snuggled beneath the blankets on the single bed in the spare room at Eric's elderly relative's, "No small sister fidgeting around like a demented puppy."

Scarlett liked Eric's grandmother, and she loved London. It had been her first trip and she was captivated by the hustle and bustle. So different to the sleepy little Essex village she came from. She toyed with the idea of suggesting to Eric that they moved closer to the city after they were married and then thought of her family and realised that she couldn't do it. Her family were her life's breath and there was no way she could bear to live so far away from them. She smiled to herself in the darkness. Even Nita, pest that she was, was part of her past and part of her soul.

It was the Sunday evening after they got back that Eric approached Dan. Scarlett and Eric were in the front room after a scene at the tea table in which Scarlett complained about having to share her evenings with the rest of the family when they must all realise she and Eric wanted to be alone.

It was unusual for Scarlett to lose her temper with her mother but on this occasion the discussion got quite heated. Maureen didn't want the best room used every day and Scarlett wanted some privacy. In the end Dan intervened.

"Come now, Maureen, what harm's it going to do, eh? They're only going to sit and listen to the radio."

If it was rare for Scarlett and Maureen to fall out, it was even rarer for Dan to intervene and Maureen knew the decision had been made.

"Well, mind you both take your shoes off before you go in there. We don't want dirt on the carpets do we?" Having had the final word she dropped the subject and Scarlett and Eric duly went into the front room after tea. Maureen couldn't settle and was for ever calling through to ask them if they wanted a drink or going through to put things in the side-board that Dan knew full well had never belonged in there before.

"For goodness sake, woman, leave them be." Maureen opened her mouth to protest and then caught her husband's eye.

"Come and sit by me." Dan patted the sofa and Maureen went and curled up beside him, putting her hand in his large strong hand.

"I know what you're worried about. You think they'll get up to all sorts on their own in that front room don't you?" He didn't wait for an answer. "And I know why, it's because you've got a long memory and can remember very what we were like in *your* Mum's house."

Maureen blushed and said nothing, but she felt a warm glow creep over her as she recalled their courting days. Dan kissed her forehead.

"That gives me an idea..."

"Oh, Dan, we can't." Maureen looked horrified.

"And why not, for goodness sake? Those two will be wrapped up in each other for hours, and Nita won't be home until half past eight-"

There was a knock on the door leading through to the small hall that divided the rooms and Eric walked in, closely followed by Scarlett.

"Dad, Eric's got something to say to you."

"Yes, Eric?" Dan looked up expectantly.

"Well, Sir ...er ...Mr. Evans, sir..."

"Get on with it," Scarlett hissed, prodding him from behind.

Dan stifled a grin.

"Well, it's like this, sir, I want to marry Scarlett." The words seemed to fall over themselves in their haste to escape from Eric's mouth.

"Do you now? Well, well."

"Come on, Dan, it's not exactly unexpected, is it?" Maureen got up and went and put her arm round her daughter who was hovering excitedly in the background.

"Well, Dad, what do you say?"

Dan stood up. "I say it's fine by me. That'll be one less mouth for me to feed."

"Oh, Dad!" Scarlett laughed and threw herself into her father's open arms.

"I think this calls for a celebration." Dan looked at Maureen. "Haven't we got a bottle of sherry hidden away for such an occasion as this?"

"I do believe we have, I'll go and fetch it."

When Maureen returned, Dan, Scarlett and Eric were sitting round the table.

"We're going to get the ring after Christmas," Scarlett was saying, "Eric thought we might be able to buy it in the January Sale," she flashed a smile at Eric, who appeared smug with his thriftiness at suggesting they purchase the ring at a reduced price.

"The engagement will be official next month," Scarlett continued, "On the 22nd as it's Eric's Mum and Dad's wedding anniversary. We thought it would be nice."

"I'm not sure that's such a good idea, " Dan said quietly.

"Oh Dad, why not?"

"Have you forgotten that it's also Nita's birthday? It would be a shame to take the limelight away from her, now wouldn't it? Surely you remember how important birthdays are when you're eleven?"

Scarlett looked dejected. "Yes, of course I do. I thought it might be nice to do it on Nita's birthday, but if you think she'd be disappointed the of course we'll change the date. Won't we, Eric?"

Eric looked embarrassed. "Yes, of course we will. Don't want to start off with trouble in the family do we? Why not make it the day we get the ring?"

"Oh yes, that would be smashing." Scarlett clapped her hands.

"And when are you two planning to get wed?" Dan asked.

"Sometime towards the end of next year, I hope." Eric said, taking his glasses off and polishing them. He squinted across at Dan; "I shall have a rise in the spring so we'll be able to put a little more away each week.   We've saved quite a bit already," he finished proudly.

When Nita came in she was told the good news and even given a small glass of sherry. She thought the sherry was vile and tipped it down the sink when nobody was looking then stood with her empty glass in her hand looking round at her family. Scarlett was over the moon tonight and who could blame her? Eric may not be everyone's cup of tea but he was what Scarlett wanted and she'd got him. He looked slightly less like a timid sparrow tonight and a bit more like a wise old owl or maybe not like a bird at all, more like the cat that got the cream.   Mum was smiling and laughing and Dad.... ell, Dad was Dad.

Nita knew she was lucky. She had a family that loved her and that she loved. One or two of her friends weren't so lucky and at this moment she felt aware of what they were missing. She was sorry when it was time to go to bed and she was packed off up the stairs, leaving the warmth of the living room, warmth caused as much by the glow of love than the open fire that crackled in the grate.

Nita's favourite Christmas present that year was a train set, which she immediately set up in her play-room. Eric bought Scarlett a headscarf and she returned his gift with a pair of socks explaining to the rest of the family that they had agreed only to buy a token present so that they could save up to get married. Dan gave Maureen a silk blouse that he had saved all year to buy, and Maureen gave him a jumper she had knitted and a new dressing gown.

Christmas had arrived with Nita still unaware of that her best friend was soon to leave the village. Richard and Anne Davidson had decided not to tell their daughter of the move until everything was signed and sealed, reasoning correctly that the idea of leaving the friends she had known all her young life would upset Sue, at least initially.

At the Big House the Davidsons had opened their presents and were playing a game of Snakes and Ladders. Ann was wishing Richard would cheer up a bit and Richard was wishing he could be anywhere but here. Sue was beginning to notice that her Father wasn't very happy these days, and wondered what she'd done now to upset him.

***

In her cottage at the other side of the village, Daphne had spent as much time on the preparation for Christmas as if she had a husband and ten children. The decorations were up, the tree decorated with tiny little golden balls, which sparkled in the glow of the fairy lights. Beneath the tree was a mass of presents for Leo. Of them all, only two were not from her. These were from his friends - one from Nita and Sue, neither of whom Daphne really knew, and one from Leo's friend, Benny.

It was an unusual friendship, Daphne thought. Her son, with the mind of a six year old unless it was anything to do with his knowledge of Westerns, in which case he could quote the author, the year of publication (or release, if it was a film), the characters and the full story line - and Benny, the appointed leader of the village children, the first one to get into scrapes, a big giant of a lad. Daphne had first met him when Leo had taken a tumble in the street and Benny had seen him home safely. On that occasion Daphne was too concerned about her son to take any notice of his companion but, when Benny called the next day to see if Leo was well enough to go out and play, Daphne invited him in to wait while Leo got his coat and shoes on, and a tentative friendship was formed between the lonely woman and the surprisingly sensitive boy.

Daphne had lived in the village for eight years now. When Derek had left her for another woman, he had given her the option of remaining in the house they had shared, or of moving away completely, into a house which he would buy.

The second option gave Daphne more dignity; she could move into a new area and nobody need know she had been unable to keep a husband; nobody would look at her with pity when she walked down the street. As a widow she would have some status.

She had decided to move to Essex, and had found the perfect place, just big enough for her and her son. Derek had paid for the cottage and, each month, had money paid directly into the bank for her and Leo to live on. She thought it ironic that her family had thrown her out when she had fallen for what they considered a nobody, somebody far beneath them on the social scale, but in the end Derek was worth more money than they were. The big house she had grown up in had taken all the family's money, and by the time her father had died he had been penniless. The house had been sold for a pittance, and what money there was left after the debts had been paid had been divided between her two brothers and her older sister, all of whom, according to her Father, had made better marriages than she had.

She hadn't begrudged them a penny of it.

Now she and her son sat beside the fire in preparation for the usual present opening ritual. Daphne poured a glass of sherry for herself, and some fizzy lemonade for Leo, opened the box of chocolates and began handing out the presents.

The pile of wrapping paper grew as treasures were unwrapped. As always, there were the usual new clothes for Leo and, in addition to her normal gifts of shirts and trousers, Daphne had bought her son a complete cowboy outfit, which Leo immediately insisted on wearing. Some thought had gone into the present from Sue and Nita, Daphne noted, and they had managed to find a book on the Wild West that Leo didn't already have. Daphne guessed they must have questioned him endlessly to eliminate the possibility of a duplicate.

Benny and she had discussed Benny's present for Leo and the result was a long cylinder wrapped in red and green paper.

As Leo unwrapped it carefully, Daphne watched her son's face and felt that all the worry and the struggle of existing on her own had been worth it. All the sacrifices she'd made to make Christmas special were rewarded as she watched her son's eyes and the look of pleasure on his face.

She hadn't seen the picture before, only heard of it, and was surprisingly impressed with the end result.

She had no idea where Benny had managed to get such a large sheet of paper; but gazing from it was Leo. An adult Leo, this, straight from the Wild West. Somehow Benny had managed to create the illusion that the gun in his hand had been pulled at a startling speed and that this Sheriff would put up with no nonsense from any outlaws.

Leo was thrilled, and the picture had to be taken immediately and stuck with drawing pins on the back of the bedroom door.

Mother and son stood together, admiring the picture. "Will I look like that one day?" Leo looked at his mother and she returned his gaze fondly.

"I daresay you will." She patted his head, a gesture she knew he hated but sometimes it just got the better of her. He ducked from under her hand and out of the door.

Daphne followed him and made her way through to the kitchen to check on the turkey.

"What's Benny and his Dad doing for Christmas?" she asked. Desmond Palmer was a widower, and Daphne knew that he and Benny usually spent Christmas with Benny"s Aunt and her family. Daphne assumed they were doing the same this year.

"They're staying at home," Benny replied, "I think his Aunt Gladys has gone away or something." Suddenly his eyes lit up as a thought struck him.

"Could we ask them here, do you think? They could have dinner with us."

"Don't be silly, Leo, they'll be cooking their own dinner."

"I could go and see, Mum." Leo jumped up excitedly, "It would be great, wouldn't it?"

Daphne definitely did not think it would be great. She discouraged people from becoming friendly, and she was quite sure that Desmond Palmer would have a multitude of things he'd rather be doing than spending time with her and Leo. It was hard to disappoint her son, but it would have to be done.

"Leave it, Leo. They won't want to come here."

"Yes they would," Leo was practically jumping up and down now with excitement at his wonderful scheme. "Benny was saying how boring Christmas would be. They'd love to come here, honest they would."

Daphne wished she hadn't brought the subject up now; she was beginning to fear she wouldn't be able to get out of it.

"We'll see," she said. "Let's have dinner, just the two of us like always, then we'll think about asking them for tea. Is that all right?"

Leo agreed, albeit reluctantly, and went off to play with his new toys and books. Daphne rather hoped that he'd forget about Benny and his Dad, but she knew her son well, and guessed it was highly unlikely.

***

At the village store Joe and Hannah Hughes were making the most of one of their few days off. Hannah had managed to prepare most of the vegetables for dinner the previous day, and now she was sitting sipping a coffee at the kitchen table, absent-mindedly stroking the dog's head where it rested on her lap, her eyes scanning the pages of the magazine on the table in front of her.

Joe was in the lounge, asleep, and Hannah let him doze on. He deserved it; the run up to Christmas had been hectic, and now was time for him to relax. They had both been up early, and walked across the road for morning Communion in the Church. Here they had exchanged greetings with friends and customers and had returned home to a breakfast of toast, dripping with butter and prepared by their daughter, Shirley, while they were gone. Shirley was in her room now, hopefully keeping an eye on young Simon, the baby of the family. Hannah smiled; at five years old she supposed Simon was no longer a baby. but she didn't intend to let him grow up too quickly.

***

Scarlett and Eric had Christmas dinner with her family and then went off to Eric's parents for tea.

"Just think," said Eric as they left, "This time next year we might be able to have you all to ours for Christmas day."

Maureen told him that would be nice and Dan grunted. Nita screwed up her face at the thought of it, the idea of not spending Christmas at home with all her presents was too terrible to think of. She went and took a jigsaw from the neat pile of presents beside the living room door. Fetching a tray from the kitchen, she settled in the big armchair opposite Dan.

"This is the way to spend Christmas, isn't it, lass?" Dan said as he bent forward and stoked the fire.

"That's easy for you to say," said Maureen as she entered the room, "You're not the one who has to cook the dinner and wash up afterwards."

"No, you're right. I'm sorry, I just didn't think." Dan sat back in his chair and smiled at his wife. "Maybe next year we *will* spend Christmas with the youngsters. It will give you a nice break.

Nita groaned and Dan shot her a warning look.

"Actually," Maureen said as she sat in the remaining chair, "I'm not sure that I want to spend Christmas away from home, and it really wouldn't be fair on Nita."

Nita nodded her agreement and her mother went on, "And I love the afternoons. Just to sit in front of the fire and know that all I've got left to do is make some sandwiches at teatime. It's one time I can relax."

"I'll tell you what," suggested Dan, "How about if Nita and I wash up the tea things for you?"

Nita looked up and began to protest but Maureen interrupted her.

"Don't worry, Nita, there'll only be the teacups and side-plates. It'll probably take you all of five minutes."

Satisfied, Nita returned her attention to the jigsaw.

"Why don't we try out your new game?" Dan asked. Nita had been given a game of Monopoly by her Aunt Erin, a fairy-godmother type figure that she had never met but who produced magnificent presents at the appropriate time.

"I was going to wait until David and Jenny came round, they'll be here about four."

"That's right, I'd forgotten," Maureen said, "Tom and Helen are coming round too. Maybe we could get the sherry out Dan?"

Dan obediently went and fetched the bottle from the sideboard.

"Looks like we'll have to get another bottle of this soon, what with the celebrations we've been having."

The doorbell rang at that moment and their neighbours, the Jermain family, entered, bringing a hint of the chill east wind with them.

It was handy having friends next door but Jenny, at thirteen, was beginning to grow away from the group they usually played with. It confused Nita. Sometimes Jenny was Miss High and Mighty and wouldn't lower herself to play with them, then another day she would be as silly as the rest of them.

"It's her age," explained Maureen when Nita complained to her, "Jenny doesn't know if she's a child or a woman and she's reluctant to leave childhood behind and hasn't yet learnt how to become a woman. You'll be just the same in a few years.

Nita doubted it but kept quiet.

David, Jenny and Nita sat at the table and Nita brought out the Monopoly. Jenny declared she was expert at it, having played it at a friends house, and it was decided that she would teach them on the grounds that would be easier than fighting their way through the rules. Dan, passing the table twenty minutes later, found it a mite suspicious that Jenny already owned two sets of properties with a hotel on each, while David and Nita couldn't even make up a set between them. He said as much and Nita saw a look settle on Jenny's face. She was beginning to know that look. It was a look that said, "I'm an adult too now, and I won't be spoken to like a child."

Before Jenny could spoil the happy atmosphere of the day, Nita closed the board with a snap, scattering hotels and playing pieces over the table.

"I'm bored with it, anyway, let's do something else."

Recognising his daughter's diplomatic move for what it was, Dan left them to it.

"How about a trip to Hill House?" David suggested.

"Oh, no, it's much too far. It'll be dark before we get there," Jenny complained.

"What's up? Scared the witch will get you?" David taunted his sister. It was legend amongst the children that a wicked witch lived in Hill House, the big house overlooking the village, and the gargoyles on the roof and door knocker only added to the illusion.

"I am not. Anyway, look who's talking. Who thought the ghosts were after him when we went into the McDonald place?"

The McDonalds hadn't lived in the house since before David and Nita were born, but it was still known as their place. No one quite knew who owned it, and it was the scene of many childhood dares. In places the roof had caved in and all the village children were forbidden by their parents to go there, but they all did.

Some of the couples who got in there were not so young and at least one unwanted pregnancy had originated from the McDonald place.

"Well, there was something there."

"Yes. The Macey's cat. But you didn't wait to find out what it was, did you cry-baby?"

"Let's just go for a walk up to the farm," Nita butted in.

It seemed a safe occupation and the three of them donned duffel coats, scarves and mittens and went on their way. By the time they got back, the snow had begun to fall, so that the dusk seemed later, lit by the white fluffs of cotton wool falling from the sky.

CHAPTER THREE

The dinner things cleared away and washed up, Daphne settled in the chair by the fire and prepared to snooze, confident that Leo would be happy reading in his bedroom for the rest of the day.

She was just nodding off when he walked into the living room.

"Are you going to ask Benny and his Dad to tea?"

Damn! He *hadn't* forgotten. He hadn't mentioned the subject since before dinner and she was beginning to think it had slipped his mind. She should have known better.

"All right then. It won't be much, mind, just some sandwiches and cake."

"It'll be great, Mum, thanks." Leo was already in the hall and putting his coat on. "I'll pop over and ask them now, shall I?"

"Don't be long then, and be careful."

"Yes, Mum, Back soon."

The door closed behind him and Daphne sighed. For the first time since she'd lived in the village she was going to have another adult in her home. She would have to make small talk, be polite and friendly but all the time being careful not to give away her secret. To avoid that, she tried to keep herself aloof from the other villagers, living her life for her son, spending her time quietly at home, indoors where she kept the place spotless, or in the garden, where all the flowers grew in regimented straight lines and where the grass was always clipped and neat.

Now all that might change.

Desmond Palmer was surprised and strangely touched when young Leo came and knocked on the door with the invitation. Young Benny had spoken highly of Leo's mother, but Des had never had the chance to make her acquaintance. Occasionally he would see her in the village, but she always struck him as not being the kind of woman you'd speak to unless you had been introduced: Which is why the invite came as such a surprise. He knew from local gossip that she was not a friendly woman, and wondered what had prompted this uncharacteristic holding forth of the Olive Branch. He decided it must be the season and, with not a little trepidation, told Leo that the Palmers would be happy to go and share Daphne and Leo's Christmas tea.

"We'll come over in about half an hour, Leo, is that all right? I'll need to have a bit of a wash first," he explained.

"Can I wait?"

"Best not, lad, your Mum might wonder where you are. Nip off home and let her know we'll be over soon."

Desmond watched until Leo was out of the gate and then closed the door thoughtfully. He felt that he ought not to visit empty handed, but couldn't think of anything in the house that might be suitable as a small gift. He'd only received handkerchiefs and socks for Christmas himself, and they would hardly be right. In the end he went into the garden and cut some winter jasmine.   Benny was pleased with the invitation. Christmas Day at home was a bit dull, his Dad had fallen asleep right after lunch and left Benny to do the washing up, after which he'd gone and sat by the fire with his new book of jokes and sat, chuckling, until Leo's ring at the door woke his Dad up.

They arrived on Daphne's door promptly half an hour later. Leo came and opened it and they followed him through to the small but cosy sitting room.

Daphne got up from the armchair when they came in and held out her hand. "Hello, I'm Daphne Taylor, thank you for coming at such short notice."

"Desmond Palmer," he shook her cool fingers, "Or Des, as I prefer to be called. And the pleasure is ours, Mrs. Taylor, we were twiddling our thumbs wondering what to do, weren't we lad?"

Benny resisted pointing out that his father had been asleep and Daphne told Des not to call her Mrs. Taylor, that Daphne would be fine. She took the flowers Des offered awkwardly, as though, Des thought, she didn't often receive gifts. Still, she seemed genuinely pleased at the gesture and put them in a crystal vase on the mantelpiece, where the yellow flowers spoke of spring and the coming year.

"Shall I make a cup of tea, Mum," Leo said eagerly.

"Be careful, then." Daphne nodded at Leo and he went out to the kitchen, closely followed by Desmond.

"Please sit down, Des," Daphne indicated the chair by the fire as she sat down again.

There was an uncomfortable silence, broken only by the crackling of the logs on the fire. Des watched his companion as she stared into the fire, seemingly oblivious to his presence. He had never seen her this closely before, and was impressed with the way she looked. Even for a day at home she was dressed smartly. Her clothes didn't look new, but they seemed to his untrained eyes, quality. Her hair was immaculately styled, and her flawless skin was free of blemishes. The only make-up was a touch of lipstick, and her only jewellery a pair of pearl stud earrings.

Suddenly she seemed aware of his presence.

"I'm sorry," she said, "I was dreaming."

"Ah, yes," he said, understandingly, "Christmas is a time of memories, isn't it?"

He thought she looked at him a little strangely before replying. "Is it? Yes, I suppose it is."

Undoubtedly she was reluctant to talk of her memories. Maybe she hadn't come to terms with being a widow yet. Strange, he himself drew great comfort from talking about Margaret, though she'd been gone several years now, it seemed like only yesterday that she'd been there beside him. Still, it seemed as though the present might be a safer topic than the past.

"Young Leo pleased with his picture?" he asked.

"Oh, yes, he was thrilled. We've hung it in his bedroom. I had no idea Benny was such a talented artist."

"Oh, yes, chip off the old block, my lad."

"Oh?"

"Well, I wouldn't want to boast now, but I'm not averse to a bit of drawing myself, although I like to stick to charcoals. Sketches of animals, old people, that sort of thing."

"Really, how interesting." Daphne actually sounded interested and he warmed to his subject, telling her of the locations he'd been to, of the antics some of the animals he'd sketched had got up to and of the fascinating conversations he'd had with some of the elderly folk that he'd sketched.

When the boys came in with the tea tray Benny was pleased to see his Dad getting on so well with Daphne. He'd felt sorry for his Dad since Mum died; he knew there'd been hard times, times when his Dad had felt lonely. Once in a while one of the women in the village would come and baby-sit and his Dad would get out for a drink or to the theatre, but these times were few and far between. For some time now he'd harboured a dream that his Dad and Leo's Mum might get together but he couldn't persuade his Dad to ask Mrs. Taylor over, and Leo's Mum never gave invitations to anybody from what he could see, so today's invitation had come like the answer to a prayer.

The adults remained chatting in their places by the fire while Leo and Benny sat at the dining table playing Beat Your Neighbour

Later Daphne made sandwiches and fresh tea and opened a tin of fruit for tea. The Christmas cake came out and was tucked into with gusto.

"I'm afraid cake isn't something I bother with," Des admitted, "So this is an extra special treat."

Daphne persuaded him to have two more pieces before he declared himself stuffed. The adults washed up while the boys continued with their card games and then Daphne got out the Monopoly and all four of them played. Leo was the winner, thanks to everyone else's help, and, as Daphne stood on the doorstep watching her guests leave, she had to admit to herself that she hadn't enjoyed a Christmas Day so much for years.

***

Mary Soames, the matriarch of Hill House, had enjoyed Christmas Day, but it had left her exhausted. At 82 years old she was beginning to feel her age and having her younger son and his family join the household for the day had been a lot for what she was beginning to think of as her 'frail old body' to cope with.

In truth Mary was a lively figure, troubled only with occasional flares of arthritis. Her older son and daughter-in-law who shared Hill House with her tended to treat her with cotton wool and Mary was not above making the most of this attention and allowing them to look after her. However, sometimes they irritated her when they suggested that she was not capable of carrying out certain simple chores that she enjoyed doing and this would occasionally spark off a family row from which Mary inevitably emerged as the winner.

At seven thirty she made her way to her bedroom where she switched on her wireless and put a few extra coals on the fire. Then she sat in her rocking chair and lost herself in memories of Christmas past.

***

Boxing Day was bright and cold and Nita wrapped up well before going to knock for David and Jenny. The snow that had looked so promising the night before had petered out during the night, leaving the odd patch of white at the base of the hedgerows.

The three of them walked in single file along the road to the village; there was no footpath and road safety had been drummed into all the village children. As they drew abreast of the Church Nita caught sight of Sue amid a group of children on the village green. She quickened her steps and David and Jenny fell behind.

"Sue," she called when she was near enough for Sue to hear her. Sue's blonde head whipped round, and, seeing Nita, she detached herself from the group and ran towards her friend. Sue never walked anywhere if she could run.

"Hi," she said, slightly breathlessly as she arrived at Nita's side. "Did you have a good day yesterday?"

"Terrific. How about you?"

"Smashing. What presents did you get?"

The two girls swapped news of the previous day's events until they were disturbed by Leo.

"Have you read-" he began before Sue interrupted him.

"Oh, Leo, *don't...*"

They both liked Leo but they couldn't make him understand that neither of them had the slightest interest in tales of the Wild West. It was Leo's consuming passion and he always started off a conversation with a discussion of the latest book he'd acquired or the latest TV series.

"Sorry." He looked sheepish and then brightened up as he remembered. "We're all going up to Hill House. Coming?"

Nita and Sue looked at each other and Nita spoke for both of them.

"Sure."

It was a game they never tired of. They would climb the steep hill and walk past the house that stood on the bend in the hill. Then they would double back across the fields and see who could dare to get closest to the house. The last time they'd tried it, David had nearly reached the back door when it had begun to open and they'd all fled. They were convinced they must have been seen and waited for repercussions in the form of complaints to their parents, but none came.

As they walked up the hill, the group of children split into subgroups. Jenny, Benny and Leo led the way, then came Shirley, Imelda and David, followed by Nita, and Sue. The only one left out was Simon. Shirley was supposed to look after her brother, but was consistently lax in her duties. Consequently Simon dawdled along behind them and occasionally Nita and Sue would have to stop and wait for him. Simon was an attractive child, too pretty for a boy, Nita always thought. She was disturbed by Shirley's lack of interest in her brother. Nita had heard her mother describe Shirley as irresponsible and was beginning to understand what the word meant. She liked Shirley, but would never dare to be as disobedient as her friend who was always late home and deliberately doing things that Hannah and Joe had expressly forbidden. Nita felt herself colour. She was not always totally obedient herself.

They passed Hill House and carried on up the hill until they rounded the second bend. Here they made their way through the trees, dead twigs snapping beneath their feet. Leo, the animal lover, caught a glimpse of brown fur and thought it was a weasel or stoat, but it had vanished before anyone else saw it.

Emerging from the far side of the trees, they made their way round the field, hugging the hedge. This meant they were out of sight of even the upstairs windows of Hill House although if Farmer Dickson cared to look out of his windows at Fable Farm with a pair of binoculars, he would have seen a rare assortment of young people skulking across the edge of one of his fields.

They reached the hole in the hedge and, one by one, sidled through it. It came out behind one of the many outbuildings in the grounds of Hill House. Some weeks previously Nita, David and Sue had actually been brave enough to enter the shed, expecting to find a wealth of treasures. They had been disappointed to find only a rusted old wheelbarrow and bucket and a pair of garden shears. There was something special about the smell though, Nita thought. Had she been older and more widely read, she might have described it as evocative. Instead, she was just aware of being reminded of the good feeling she got when she was in her father's shed in their garden at home. Sometimes, on rainy summer days, she would take a chair and a book and an apple and go and sit in Dan's shed and she relished the feeling of being snug and dry and secluded that the shed gave her.

As usual, most of the girls hung back now with the exception of Nita, who hated to be left out of anything.

Jenny and Imelda felt themselves too old for such escapades, why they were there at all was a mystery to Nita, and Sue and Shirley were just plain scared so they were elected to look after Simon and try and keep him quiet.

Between the outbuilding and the house were other sheds and some high hedges, which afforded good cover for quite some way. Then there was a strip of lawn of about twenty yards, which was completely open. David had been crossing this area on the last occasion when the door had opened.

None of the children had ever considered what they would do if they reached the house. Maybe today they'd find out.

They carefully picked their way through the rough areas between the sheds until they came to the clearing.

"I'm not going first again," David stated, "I went first last time."

"Okay," said Benny, "I'm oldest, I'll go."

Behind the sheds Shirley chose that moment to hit Simon who she thought had trodden on her toe. He had indeed, but it had been an accident and Simon thought the slap that Shirley gave him was unwarranted and uncalled for. He duly let out an anguished wail and the group by the lawn froze. Inside the house a dog barked.

"Strewth," said Benny, "Sounds fierce."

"Aren't you going across now, then?" Nita was disappointed.

Benny felt awkward. He didn't want to admit he was scared.

"Let's go and see what the rest of them think," he suggested.

They re-grouped behind the sheds where Simon's sobs had now subsided to a grizzle.

"He'll keep that up for ages," Shirley said, "We might as well give up and go home."

Nita secretly thought that Benny looked rather relieved although he voiced his disappointment.

"I've never seen the witch," she said, "I was hoping today I would."

"Oh, she's nothing special." Shirley had been with her father once when he had delivered some groceries to Hill House, and had caught a brief glimpse of the elderly figure dressed all in black that opened the door. Curiously, it had never occurred to any of the children to question their parents about the witch although they knew that some of them must have had contact with her. It was as though they secretly suspected it was only the young that knew the truth about the occupant of Hill House.

Still," Nita said now, "It would have been nice to see for myself. Never mind," she added philosophically, "There's always another day."

The group made their way reluctantly back down the hill to the village green where they went their separate ways. Nita went back to the Big House with Sue, and Richard Davidson later took her home in the car of which he was so proud and Dan so envious.

***

It was the beginning of January before Richard and Ann had confirmation that the sale of their house had gone through. Contracts were signed and it was time to begin packing in earnest. Ann had already packed up things that were seldom used and the loft was full of neatly piled cardboard boxes.

But first there was Sue to be told.

"Richard should have been here," Ann thought as she looked at her daughter's face and at her eyes, which were filled with tears, tears that were beginning to spill over the edges and run down Sue's smooth, creamy skin.

Ann didn't know what to say. It hadn't occurred to her or Richard that Sue wouldn't want to move. Although they realised that she might be unsettled by the prospect, they thought the excitement of going to a new, modern house would overcome that.

"I've been so selfish," Ann said, putting her arms round her daughter and drawing her near, "I've been so thrilled about going to live in a town with a nice modern house, that it never occurred to me you wouldn't be pleased as well."

"But I'll have to leave my friends," Sue wailed, "What about Nita, and Shirley and the rest of them. And I'll have to go to a new school where I won't know anyone and they'll all be horrid to me and I'll get left out of all the games." She groped in her pocket for her handkerchief.

"It won't be for long, you know," Ann said as she stroked her daughter's blonde head, "You'll soon make new friends. And after the summer you'd be going to a new school anyway. We're not going to the end of the world, after all. You'll have to write to Nita and Shirley, and maybe they'll be able to come and stay with us during the holidays."

Sue sniffed. "I'm sorry, Mum, I just don't want to go. I don't want to leave my bedroom, I don't want to sleep somewhere strange."

"You silly girl," Ann said kindly, "It will be much nicer. Because the house is smaller, it will be warmer, and you'll still have everything of yours in your bedroom. Tell you what, how about we make yours the first room to decorate and you choose the wallpaper?"

It was the best thing Ann could have said. The idea of choosing her own decor certainly appealed to Shirley.

"How many bedrooms are there?" Sue was interested now, and wanted to make sure the house was big enough for when her friends came to stay.

"There's three. One for Dad and me, and one for you, and a spare one. Downstairs there's a living room and dining room and kitchen. Hey, where are you going?"

Sue was nearly out of the room already. She turned and looked at her mother.

"I've got to go and tell Nita. I'll be back in time for lunch."

"Don't forget your coat," Ann called and, hearing the bang of the front door closing, glanced out of the window. Sue was running down the drive putting her coat on as she went. Ann breathed a sigh of relief. It was going to be all right.

CHAPTER FOUR

New Year's Eve had passed quietly for most of the villagers with the possible exception of the men in the public bar of The Red Lion.

The following morning Harry Miles woke up at ten o'clock in the bedroom of his terraced house adjacent to the pub. He tried to sit up and found the throbbing in his head was too much to bear, so he sank back down into his pillows again. Must have tied on one too many last night, he thought, remembering that he'd spent the evening with the lads in the Red Lion.

His wife, Belinda, was in the bathroom, trying to disguise the fresh bruise appearing on her cheek; she had intended going to Church for the eleven o'clock service, but she was developing a shiner. There was no point in giving the rest of the village more fuel for their speculations about the state of her marriage.

Elsewhere in the village other men were suffering the effects of a heavy drinking session the previous night, but of their wives and women, only Belinda Miles suffered physically as a result.

At three o'clock she called her husband for his dinner. He put his dressing gown on over the underwear he had not bothered to strip off the night before and made his way to the kitchen table. Belinda knew better than to tell Harry that the aroma he gave off was stronger than the sage and onion stuffing, but she kept as far apart from him as she could. The fumes on his breath were enough to light a fire, she thought, and the vomit staining his vest gave off a sickly sweet odour. After he'd eaten he went and sat in the living room, where she let him fall back to sleep while she washed up in the cheerless scullery. She wondered if she dared slip out and see Martha for half an hour, but knew if he woke up and found her gone there'd be hell to pay, so she put her own desires to one side and sat on the sofa, a bag of sewing at her side.

***

Eric and Scarlett went to Colchester to buy the engagement ring on the first Saturday in the New Year. It was decided that there would be no party, relatives and friends would be advised of the engagement by letter. Eric felt it was best not to waste the money on frivolity, Scarlett told her parents, and Maureen secretly congratulated her daughter on having found such a careful partner.

"I suppose you think I'm extravagant?" Dan complained later that night when she voiced her opinions aloud as they were preparing for bed.

"Don't be daft, man, you know I'd never accuse you of that, but don't you agree that it's nice we won't have to worry about our Scarlett marrying an idle lay-about who only wants to spend money and won't put himself out to earn it?"

"Of course, dear, of course. Nonetheless, I'd have liked there to be a bit more generosity in the man. Do you know how much that ring cost?"

"No, I don't. It's none of our business," Maureen said firmly.

"No, you're right," Dan sighed, "Still, it would have been nice to have actually had a diamond large enough to see without a magnifying glass."

"Dan Evans, that's enough." Maureen turned from her position on the stool in front of the mirror to face her husband. "The boy was ready enough with his money when we were at the restaurant this evening wasn't he?"

"Oh, yes, he got that silly little purse out, but not until I'd told him the meal was on us. After all, it was the least we could do. It's not every day our daughter gets engaged, is it?"

Maureen got up from the stool and came and sat on the Dan's side of the bed. He put his arm round her.

"No, it's not." She leaned her head on his shoulder, "I'd have liked to have done more for them, given them a party or something, but I really believe they preferred the money to a present."

"Yes, I think you're right. Anyway, they seem happy enough." He drew back and gazed at her. "And it's made you happy, hasn't it?"

She nodded, "And I can tell you someone else who's a lot happier these days...."

"Oh? And who might that be?"

"Desmond Palmer," Maureen declared triumphantly. "And I know why."

"Oh? So what is it you know my little gossip?"

"I know that Desmond Palmer had been seeing rather a lot of Daphne Taylor."

"Has he now? And where did you pick that little snippet of information up from?"

"Hannah told me. Apparently it's the talk of the village."

Dan wasn't surprised to hear that the information came from Hannah. Everyone in West Morling passed through the door of the village stores sooner or later and it was a natural meeting place for a gossip. Living half a mile outside of the village Maureen had to wait for her evening stint in the shop before picking up the latest news. Not that she was really a gossip, nothing she learned in the shop went further than her own bedroom; Maureen was a natural keeper of secrets and was often sought out by friends to be the recipient of the snippets of information they just couldn't keep to themselves.

Dan knew, as Maureen did, that it would only have been necessary for Des Palmer to go through Daphne Taylor's garden gate once for the village to have enlarged it into the romance of the century but he couldn't deny that he'd like to see Des with a lady in his life again, it must have been hard for him, raising that boy of his on his own.

"Ah well, I suppose we'll just have to wait and see what develops," Dan said, watching his wife as she sat by the mirror, "Now, are you coming to bed, or have I got to wait even longer?

***

Martha Skingsley sat on the window-seat in her bungalow and watched the life of the village go by. She had seen the children group together and go off on some adventure of their own and was reminded of times in her childhood when she had met her friends in exactly the same place on the village green. Now her friends had all grown and left the village, some of them had died in foreign fields during the War and some of them had died at home of natural and some of not so natural causes.

Martha had continued to live in the village, caring for her parents until they both passed away within six months of each other, and working evenings in the village store until her arthritis forced her to give up even this contact with the outside world.

Now she watched for her friend, Belinda, hoping she would come and visit as she had promised. They got on well, these two, the old and the young; neither of them having known a lot of joy in their lives. But for Belinda there was still time; Martha wished more than anything that her young friend would give that husband of hers his marching orders and send him packing. Not that Belinda had told Martha about the beatings, but age brought wisdom and, besides, you didn't have to be particularly clever to spot the marks that were left. Harry Miles wasn't always careful about where he hit his wife.

From her position in the window looking out across the green Martha could see Belinda's house and she sat, gazing unendingly at the green door through which Belinda might appear.

Belinda, meanwhile, was not giving a passing thought to her friend, Martha. She was enjoying one of Harry's rare contrite sessions. It was for times like this, when Harry was so gentle and caring towards her, that Belinda stayed with him. That, and the fact she had no idea where she would go if she left, so she put up with the bad times, and made the most of the good.

Apparently Harry was filled with sorrow at the way he'd treated her on New Years Days. Belinda had been ordered to put her feet up and Harry had prepared the breakfast - eggs and bacon swimming in grease; had washed up and put away the crockery and cutlery and had joined her in the living room where she was dozing. He had woken her with a kiss, and had slowly, gently, brought her nerve ends alive with his loving. He wiped away all thoughts of the harsh words that passed so often between them, and Belinda forgot the beatings, forgot the amount of times she had to clear up his vomit after his drunken bouts, and gave herself over to his sweet and precious love-making.

Afterwards they lay together, Harry dropping soft kisses on her face and brushing away the damp hair that stuck to her forehead. She gazed into his eyes and wondered how long the good times would last for this time.

They lasted until mid-afternoon by which time Harry had helped prepare the dinner, had laid the table and done the washing up. When he took the bottle of whisky out of the sideboard Belinda groaned. He'd already drunk several glasses of beer with his dinner.

One hour and half a bottle later Harry declared himself sick of lazing about indoors with an ugly, boring woman. He was going out to look for better things. Ignoring Belinda's protests, he took his overcoat from the hook and, shaking her hand from his arm as she tried to prevent him leaving, left the house, slamming the door behind him.

***

It was Monday, January 6th and the last day of the Christmas holidays. Nita was up early as usual. She tended to blame Scarlett for causing her to rise early, Scarlett had to be out of the house and waiting for the bus by 8.15, so she usually rose at seven, disturbing her sister as she did so. Secretly, Nita suspected, and Scarlett was fairly positive, that Nita would wake up early anyway. Today she was up and having breakfast by the time Scarlett left the house.

"So what are you planning to do today?" Maureen, who had already been up for over two hours, asked.

Nita looked glum.

"Don't know, really, seems a shame to waste the last day of the holidays, but no one seems to have planned anything."

"Well, that's where you're wrong. Mrs. Davidson came into the shop on Friday, and suggested that Sue's Dad takes all of us into Colchester to do some shopping. I know it's a few weeks to your birthday, but I thought you might like to choose yourself some clothes as an early present."

Nita was struck dumb.

"You mean choose them myself, not have what you want?"

Maureen nodded. "Within reason, of course. I'll not let you have anything too extreme, but you're growing up now, and your Father and I think you're old enough to make some decisions on your appearance. That doesn't mean you're old enough to start wearing make-up, young lady, so don't go getting any ideas from that Shirley."

Nita was still too excited at the prospect of her new clothes to take much notice of the remark about Shirley, but when she thought about it later she realised that her Mum didn't miss much. It was true that Shirley did wear make up, but never very much, and Nita was surprised that her mother had noticed. In fact, Shirley had promised that one evening in the near future, Nita and Sue could visit and Shirley would instruct them in the art of making themselves beautiful. Actually, Nita would like to suggest to Shirley that she could do with some lessons herself. Shirley's hair, which she had an abundance of and which could have been quite exquisite, Nita thought, was always left uncombed and hanging in rats tails. Nita would love to have got her hands on Shirley's hair and given it a good brush, then braided it and pinned it up the way she did with Scarlett's sometimes.

"What time are we going?" Nita asked now.

"Don't panic, you've got plenty of time. Sue's Dad's coming for us at ten o'clock."

Nita was washed and dressed by nine-thirty and Maureen smiled to herself. Now she knew what would make her daughter get a move on in the mornings.

Nita seated herself in the parlour by the window and waited in a fever of anticipation. The trip in the motor car was exciting enough, but to actually be able to choose her own clothes - that was something else. Her thoughts strayed to shoes - was it possible...? But no, she breathed a sigh of regret, there was no way her mother would allow her to wear high heels. Even Scarlett was frowned on for that habit.

Maureen put her head round the door. "Don't you go letting your imagination run away with you, young lady. I'm not planning to spend that much money. Probably I've got enough for a couple of dresses and maybe some underwear."

Nita heard the car before she saw it and ran into the hall, "Mum, they're here," she called as she took her coat from the peg. Shrugging herself into it, she was out of the door and halfway down the path before she heard her mother's "Okay, I'm coming."

She said "Hello" to Sue's parents and then squeezed up next to Sue in the back seat, allowing room for Maureen. The two girls giggled their way to Colchester and fell out of the car, still laughing, when they reached the car park. Maureen unwound herself from the cramped position, and stretched and flexed her limbs before feeling herself relax.

Maureen and Ann and the two girls went off to the shops, arranging to meet Richard in the afternoon for the lift home.

"He's on holiday," Ann complained, "But he can't stay away from that damn bank."

"Never mind," Maureen consoled her; "You still see quite a bit of him."

Ann looked embarrassed. "Sorry, Maureen, I wasn't thinking. You and Dan don't see too much of each other, do you?"

Maureen, aware of her friend's discomfort, smiled encouragingly. "Oh, it's not too bad this time of year. Now the crops are sown and the days are short it's a little easier. It's in the summer I get lonely. Now," her tone became brisk as she changed the subject, "Where shall we head for first?"

Two hours later found the four of them settled in a café in the High Street, tucking into sticky buns. The shopping had been safely locked away in the car.

Nita was pleased with her dresses, and relieved at the ease with which she had got her own way over the choice. Maureen had put up only a token resistance at the one she complained was 'too old for you'. Nita failed to see why she should think that. Certainly the neck was cut rather low at the front, but she hadn't got any breasts yet so she couldn't see it really mattered. She loved the material, the white and yellow daisies on the bright red background and the full, flowing skirt. She had twirled round and round in the shop until the skirt stood out at right angles to her body.

"And that's another thing," Maureen had said, "It's time you started wearing a petticoat."

A petticoat had been added to the list of purchases, together with two new vests and some knickers. Nita had categorically refused to wear a bodice any longer and, again, Maureen had given in. However, Nita knew there were some things her mother would not capitulate on, so she avoided the subject of shoes, her old flat lace ups would see her through until it was warm enough for sandals.

Sue had not fared so well. Her mother had explained that with a change of school imminent, it was wise to leave the purchase of new clothes until the new uniform was acquired. Sue couldn't fault the logic and was content with new underwear which, as her mother had rightly pointed out, she would need anyway.

"We've got some time until we're due to meet Richard," Ann said, "What shall we do for the next hour or so?"

There was a slight difference of opinion as Nita wanted to visit the Natural History Museum and Sue wanted to go to the Castle because she liked the dungeons. The Castle won.

Much to Sue's disappointment the dungeons were closed, so they contented themselves with viewing the artefacts displayed in the museum. Nita found it rather boring, but she liked the feel of treading the stone floors, knowing that they had been trodden by people for centuries and she was quite impressed with the Mummy that was on show. She found it rather awesome that it contained the body of someone who had been dead thousands of years. It made her feel shivery.

At home that evening, Dan suitably admired Nita's new clothes. "You've made a good choice," he said, patting her on the head.

"Run along and hang them up now," Maureen told her, "And don't forget, you're to keep them for best. No wearing them to play in."

"Yes, Mum." Nita ran upstairs and could be heard opening and closing drawers and doors as she put away her new clothes.

"And now," Dan said, putting an arm round his wife, "What did my lady buy for herself?"

Maureen coloured at the thought of her uncharacteristic extravagance. "Actually," she admitted, "I've been completely wasteful."

Dan stood back and viewed her with a look of mock severity.

"Out with it," he demanded, "Make your confession, wench."

"Oh, Dan," Maureen laughed and he noticed again how her laugh was still that of a young girl, "You are a fool." She went out into the hall and bought back a shopping bag from which she produced a wisp of a hat. Wordlessly, she held it out for Dan's inspection.

"Hrmmph," he grunted, "Not much in that. How much did it cost? A shilling?"

Maureen grinned and shook her head.

"Two then," Dan suggested, "Surely not - not half a crown?"

Maureen put the hat on her head. The soft, lilac felt perched on her hair, with the net sweeping across her face, giving her a look of mystery. She could see that, whatever he said, Dan was captivated by it.

"Actually, Dan, it cost a fortune which we can ill afford, but I fell in love with it. I thought I could put it away for when Scarlett and Eric get wed."

Dan put his arms round her and pulled her close. He lifted the net and kissed her on the forehead.

"My love, if the hat is what you wanted then I'm thrilled to bits that you bought it. It looks divine on you and you deserve something nice."

His lips found hers and they were locked in a hungry embrace when Nita came clattering down the stairs.

"Later," Maureen promised as she pushed her husband away and, removing the hat, put it carefully back in the bag to be taken upstairs and put away. "Oh, I nearly forgot," she exclaimed, "I bought something for you."

"And there I was thinking you'd been gallivanting about all day and not giving me a thought. Ah, some socks, how thrilling."

"You know you need them," Maureen said as she handed over the thick woolly footwear, "I've darned your others so much they're all darning and no sock."

"You're quite right, my dear, and thank you very much."

Nita had come into the room and was settled in the armchair with a book with the idea that if she kept quiet enough she might remain unnoticed and therefore allowed to stay up later. Usually on the last night of the holidays an early night was the rule and today was no exception.

"Come on then," Maureen put a hand on her shoulder. "Into the kitchen with you. We'll get your hair washed and you bathed and then maybe we could have a game of cards before bed." She looked at Dan questioningly.

"Sounds good to me," he agreed.

That night, when Nita was in bed, Maureen and Dan settled in front of the fire, Maureen in the armchair with Dan on the floor, resting his head against her knees. Absent-mindedly, she stroked his hair.

"I don't think Ann's very happy," she said suddenly.

"No?" Dan turned and looked at her, "What makes you say that?"

"I don't know, just one or two things she said today. And her general attitude I suppose. Oh, she's looking forward to the move all right, but I get the

71

feeling that she hopes it's going to solve more problems than just the money situation."

"What are you suggesting?"

"I don't know really." Maureen turned Dan's head back to face the fire and resumed stroking his hair; "It's just me being fanciful. Only I was thinking..."

He turned again. "Yes?"

She bent forward and kissed him. "I'm so glad we're us, and not someone else."

He returned her kiss. "So am I, my love, so am I. And I'll be damned glad when Scarlett's in and we can go to bed."

"She'll be in soon. Just be patient a little longer. Why don't you put the radio on and I'll go and make us a drink?"

"Good idea." Dan got up and went across to the old valve radio in the corner. Once it had warmed up, he turned the dial until he found some big band music then went and resumed his place by the fire. He thought about what Maureen had said about Ann. Perhaps the rumours he'd heard had been true after all then. He'd not said anything to Maureen, not wanting to disturb her, but the blokes in the pub had been talking about Richard and one of the women he worked with having been seen in a secluded restaurant in Colchester some months previously. Dan had dismissed the rumours as rubbish, there could have been any number of explanations for Richard to be taking a colleague out to dinner and Dan wasn't one to spread rumours anyway. But now he wondered if they were true after all, if Ann had found out it would explain why they were leaving the area. Dan gave shrugged his shoulders. Lord knew some men didn't know when they were well off. He smiled at Maureen as she came in with the tray and thought again how lucky he was.

CHAPTER FIVE

"I don't know why you don't just up and leave," Martha Skingsley said as Belinda related the latest quarrel with Harry. Well, it wasn't a quarrel really, Martha reflected, more of a one-man tirade.

Belinda hadn't mentioned any punches, but Martha could see fresh red weals overlaying the fading yellow from the bruises Belinda had appeared with after Christmas.

"Well, why don't you?" Martha placed a cup of steaming coffee on the table.

Belinda looked up. "I love him," she said simply, as though that explained everything and excused all Harry's behaviour. And for Belinda it did just that. She didn't have enough imagination to envisage life without him; couldn't see past the next argument, the next beating, the next making up.

All her life there had been a man to care of her. Her Father, the Reverend George Meldreth Thomas, had ruled his household with a rod of iron until his untimely death when he and his wife were involved in an accident in their new motor car.

Belinda had already been engaged to Harry, who had charmed both her and her father round his little finger. There was no sign, as yet, of the violence that lay beneath his outward exterior, just a hint of suppressed animal magnetism which, being so alien to anything Belinda had experienced before, drew her to him like a magnet.

She never knew why Harry singled her out, didn't realise that her naivety had its own simple charm and that Harry found it a refreshing change after the worldly wise women he had grown used to.

With a rapidity that Belinda found hard to keep up with her life changed drastically after the death of her stern but fair father and the weak but affectionate mother. The wedding was brought forward with an almost unseemly haste 'so that I can take care of you, Belinda,' Harry said.

At first things had seemed all right. They had quickly settled into a routine in their marriage. If Harry was a little hard on her sometimes it was only what she was used to and she thought nothing of it.

They scarcely been married for a month the first time Harry hit her. He'd been out for a lunch time drink at the pub and the dinner wasn't quite ready when he returned home. Belinda had been late putting the vegetables on to cook, having been side-tracked talking to Sandra over the garden fence.

It was just the one punch on that occasion, and the contrition was immediate. Harry wrapped her in his arms and promised he would never, ever lay a finger on her again.

However, it set the pattern for their marriage. Gradually the beatings became more frequent and prolonged and the apologies had now all but disappeared.

"You're a fool," Martha said. Belinda looked up at her.

"I know," she said, "I know that staying with him is a foolish thing to do, but what else can I do?"

Suddenly Martha was struck by an idea so simple she couldn't understand why she hadn't thought of it before.

"You could come and live here with me," she suggested, "This place is plenty big enough for the two of us, and it would be company for me."

Belinda shook her head. "I couldn't pay my way, Martha. I've no job and no money and, besides, Harry wouldn't let me go."

"So don't tell him. Just pack your things and leave."

Belinda sighed and clipped back a stray curl of her mousy hair that had escaped from its restraint. "But don't you see, he'd know immediately where I was. Good Lord, Martha, you can see this bungalow if you glance out of our living room window, we could hardly keep my presence here quiet. Then he'd be over here throwing his weight around and demanding I go back."

Martha pulled herself up to her full 5"4".

"He'd have to get past me first," she said bravely.

Belinda laughed, a bitter sound with no humour in it.

"He'd make mincemeat of you, Martha, and you know it." She replaced the empty coffee cup in the saucer and stood up. "I'd better go, if I don't get his tea on soon it won't be ready when he comes in and there'll be more trouble." She patted the older woman on the shoulder. "Don't worry about me, Martha, I'll be all right."

Martha wasn't so sure, but there was nothing more she could do for now. She stood on her doorstep and watched sympathetically as Belinda walked slowly across the road back to her own house.

***

"Have you heard," said Joe to Hannah one morning, "The McDonald place has been sold?"

Shirley pricked up her ears. This was news indeed. She, along with the rest of the village children, looked on the McDonald place as theirs. OK, so it was too spooky to spend much time there, and you certainly wouldn't want to go there alone, but at least it was there; there for those times that you wanted to be frightened or wanted to frighten others. Now it looked as though things might be changing.

"No," Hannah replied, "I hadn't heard that. And it's unlike you, Joe Hughes, to be the bearer of gossip."

"It's not rumour, my love. Jim Elliot told me last night in the pub, and he got it from Sam Sanders. You know, him that works at the Electricity shop in town. Appears the new owners went in to enquire about having everything connected and such like."

"Well I never," Hannah sounded surprised, as indeed she was. The McDonald place had already been empty when she and Joe had moved into the village a year before Shirley was born. Still, new people in the village meant new customers for her shop. She'd make it her business to find out more about the newcomers in preparation. People liked to know you'd made an effort, she told herself, never admitting for one moment that she was just plain nosy.

Shirley couldn't wait to see Nita and Sue and tell them, but first she had to wash the breakfast things and sweep the kitchen floor, her duties for Saturday mornings. Later she'd have to help her Mum change the sheets on the bed, but that wouldn't be done until the lunch-time lull in the shop.

She called for Sue at ten o'clock, waiting in the hall while Sue got her coat and scarf from the small room the Davidsons used as a cloakroom. The hall had been stripped of its trimmings in readiness for the move to the Midlands in two weeks time.

"OK, ready." Sue took a last look in the mirror before ushering her friend out of the front door and shutting it behind her.

"I heard some news this morning," said Shirley, with the smug air of someone who knows some juicy bit of gossip; a chip off the old block, Shirley.

"Oh?" said Sue, abstractedly, deep in thoughts of her own.

"Well, don't you want to hear?"

"Oh, go on then," Sue looked at her friend intently, "What is it?"

Shirley stopped walking. This needed their full attention. "There's going to be people living in the McDonald place."

Sue hadn't halted her step. "Oh, is that all?"

"Don't you think it's a cheek? Imagine someone living there, where will we go now?"

"Oh, don't be daft. We hardly ever go there as it is. Besides, it won't much matter to me, will it?"

Sue was full of confused thoughts. In many ways she was looking forward to the move, she couldn't wait to get into a warm house, with her own, new bedroom but, as the day drew near, she began to dread leaving her old friends, and the thought of being a new girl in a new school made her quake with fear.

"You'll be all right," Nita had assured her, "Everyone will like you and you'll soon forget us."

"Oh, no. No, I'll never forget you, Nita. And I'm sure you're just being nice saying that everyone will like me."

Nothing Nita could say could convince Sue that finding new friends was going to be easy, but she supposed she was just going to have to face it head on.

"Sorry, Sue, I never thought," Shirley said now.

Sue smiled at her friend. "That's OK, it's just me feeling sorry for myself. So what else do you know about these people that are moving in?"

Shirley looked sheepish. "Nothing really. It was just something my Dad said at breakfast."

"Well, we haven't been up to the McDonald place for a while, let's go and get Nita and we'll take a trip up there now. It will almost certainly be my last chance, and probably yours as well. Race you..." and she was gone, knowing she'd have to get a head start on Shirley, whose running ability was only matched by her talent for finding out news.

They arrived at Nita's door breathless, Shirley several yards in the lead so that the door was already being opened by the time Sue got there.

"Come on in, girls," Maureen said, "Nita's in her bedroom, you might as well go straight up."

Scarlett was spending more and more time at Eric's which pleased Nita enormously as it meant she had the bedroom to herself. She was sprawled out on the bed when the two girls entered the room, crayons and pens and pencils surrounding her.

"Cor, you'll be in trouble," Shirley said, eyeing a spreading stain on the white sheet.

"Oh heck." Nita grabbed up the offending fountain pen and put the top on it. Taking a piece of blotting paper she dabbed at the ink stain until she could get no more moisture out of it. "Damn, it's going to show whatever I do. Oh, well." She pulled herself up into a sitting position and looked up at her friends. "Are you going to sit down then?" She nodded at the bed and both girls obediently seated themselves.

"How do you fancy going out?" Shirley asked.

"Not much," Nita said, "It's cold."

"Never mind that," Sue got up and went and got Nita's coat from the wardrobe. "Put this on and your gloves and scarf. We're going to the McDonald place. Tell her why, Shirley."

Shirley relayed the news and was gratified to find Nita's reaction was the same as hers had been. She, too, with the arrogance of youth, thought it a cheek that anyone would consider living in the McDonald place.

Within minutes the three friends were off down the lane.

The McDonald place was the only house down Thimble Lane and the only people that went down there, apart from the curious and the children, were people walking their dogs. The lane finished where some more of Farmer Davidson's fields began and at a point where a footpath led across to the marshy backwaters.

As they approached the McDonald place the girls became aware of changes. The sound of hammering hung on the cold winter air and, as the McDonald place came into view, they could see lights and hear the sounds of voices.

"Hey, they must be living here already," Nita said indignantly.

"I doubt it, Dad would have said," Shirley pointed out.

As they drew nearer still, they realised the house was full of workmen, repairing and decorating and making the place fit to live in. Two motor cars were in the driveway and, standing close to the car nearest the gate, were a man and a woman. They were gazing at the house and pointing things out to one another. The man was smoking a cigarette and, as he threw it to the ground, his glance rested upon the three girls, who were standing goggle eyed watching the activity.

Sue was the only one of the three who saw the man nudge his companion and point the girls out to her. Then the man took the woman's arm and led her out of the gate and along the lane.

Shirley and Nita had spotted them by this time. "Time to go, girls," said Shirley, preparing to run for it.

"Don't be daft, we're not doing anything wrong. It's a free country and we're as entitled to be standing here as anyone else." Nita was as defiant as ever.

"Well, well, well, what have we here?" The man's voice was deep and round and warm and the girls liked him straight away. "I suppose they've sent the three loveliest ladies in the village to greet us, is that right?"

The girls giggled and the woman smiled.

"Well, how about an introduction?" He held out a hand, "I'm Fred Little, and this is my wife, Josephine."

The woman held out a hand hesitantly and fluttered it in the air before returning it, untouched, to the crook of her husband's arm. "Hello," she whispered.

The girls solemnly shook Fred Little's proffered hand and returned his wife's smile.

"We also have a daughter, Caroline, but she's not with us today, she's spending the weekend with her grand-mother. She's about your age, so she'll be pleased to hear about you. Who shall I tell her you are?"

"I'm Nita, I live at the cottages on the way into the village, and this is Shirley, she lives at the village stores, and this is Sue, but she's going soon."

Fred nodded at this information. "As I expect you realise, we're buying Yew Trees here and we hope to be living here within the month. Now I think we'd better go and get on with the supervising. It's been a pleasure to meet you charming ladies, and we look forward to seeing you again. Au Revoir for now." He gave a little mock salute and, turning, led his wife back to the house.

After a minute or two of bemused silence, the girls convulsed into giggles, which they tried to stifle, not wanting to offend their new friend.

"It's been a pleasure to meet you charming ladies..." Nita mimicked, as soon as she could speak.

"...We look forward to seeing you again." Shirley continued, and they started to run towards the village green, where there was sure to be someone they could tell about their encounter.

***

Nita's birthday would be a Wednesday, and a school day, but this did not dampen her enthusiasm.

"You'll have to have your friends to tea on Saturday," Maureen warned her, "I haven't time in the week."

"That's okay, Mum, it will be better at the weekend, we can start earlier, while it's still light."

"That's right," agreed Maureen, relieved there wasn't going to be the same fuss that there had been the year before when Nita was told she couldn't have a party on her actual birthday, "There'll just be the family for tea on the day - and Eric of course."

Nita groaned. "It's not Scarlett's birthday, why do *her* friends get to come to tea?"

"Because Eric's almost one of the family now, and we have to include him at family get togethers."

"It's not fair," Nita grumbled, "It's my birthday, I should be allowed to have who I want to tea, and I definitely do not want Eric."

"You'd better be quiet, my girl, otherwise you'll end up with no party at all."

Nita decided discretion was the better part of valour and took herself out of the kitchen and back up to her room. Here she sat on the bed and made a list of the people she would invite. Her mother hadn't told her how many guests she would be allowed, but when she counted up her list, she had a sneaking feeling that

22 would be too many. Swiftly she went through and struck off the majority of the names, leaving eight. That should be okay, she thought, and she rewrote the revised list, intending to take it to school the next day, once her mother had passed it.

In the kitchen Maureen was busy making mental notes for the party in nine days time. There was plenty of time it was true, but Maureen was nothing if not organised and there was shopping to be done, and baking, plus she would have to arrange some games because it would be too cold for the children to play outside. In the end she decided to go the whole hog and book a magician. This wasn't as extravagant as it sounded; one of the women Scarlett worked with was married to a man who did a bit of magic and conjuring in his spare time. Scarlett had mentioned once before that he travelled round children's parties and Maureen thought it would be nice to have something a bit different. She decided to ask Scarlett that night to make the arrangements.

***

"Do you ever get the feeling you're being manipulated?" Des asked as he drew on his pipe.

Daphne glanced up from where she was pouring the tea at the trolley. "What on earth do you mean?"

Des took the pipe from his mouth and waved it in the general direction of Leo's bedroom. "Them two," he said, referring to the two boys who were noisily playing cards behind the closed door. "I think they're trying a bit of match-making."

"Oh, no, I'm sure you're wrong. Leo wouldn't..."

"Not Leo, perhaps, although I suspect he'd go along with anything Benny suggested, but I know Benny, and I bet you all these suggestions for us to spend time with you and Leo is based on a bit more than the boy's friendship."

Daphne felt herself colour, and her hand trembled as she passed the cup and saucer to Des. "I don't know what to say...It just hadn't occurred to me..."

"Well, whether I'm right or whether I'm wrong, I think there's something I ought to tell you."

Daphne felt her heart sink. She didn't think of Des in a romantic light at all, much as she liked him. And if he had decided to declare undying love for her, life was going to become very difficult.

Des waited until she had taken her own cup and saucer and resumed her seat before continuing.

"The truth is, Daphne, I already have a lady friend, have had for some months now. I wasn't sure how Benny would take to the idea, so I haven't told him yet and, in any case, it's been little more than a friendship up until recently so there was nothing to tell. You're a fine, attractive woman, Daphne, and under different circumstances perhaps our relationship might have developed differently, but I wanted to put you in the picture here and now so that we know where we stand. I would very much like to go on being friends, but if you'd rather we called a halt to our friendship I'll quite understand."

Daphne gave a mental sigh of relief.

"Nothing of the sort, Des," she said, " I'm very pleased for you and of course I'd like to go on being friends. Indeed, I hope once you've told Benny, that all three of you will come and see me." She placed the cup and saucer carefully on the stone hearth. "You may have realised that I don't find it easy to make friends and, whatever their motives, I'm very grateful to the boys for having engineered this friendship." She spread her hands in a suppliant gesture, "I suppose what I'm trying to say is I don't want to lose my only friend in West Morling."

Des smiled at her. "No danger of that," he promised, "In fact, I've decided you've done enough hiding away." He fumbled in his pocket and withdrew his wallet from which he extracted a couple of tickets, which he waved in the air. "Charlie's Aunt," he explained, "Even someone as reclusive as you are cannot have missed the fact that the Church acting group are putting this play on next week. I've decided we'll go on Saturday."

"Oh, no, Des, I couldn't."

"And why not?"

"Well, there's Leo and everything, I just couldn't."

"Now look, Daphne, there's no problem with Leo. Martha Skingsley was going to sit with Benny for the evening, she can just as easily come here and sit for the two lads here."

"Oh, I don't know, Des, I've nothing to wear."

"Stop making excuses, woman. You've never looked anything but immaculate in all the times I've seen you, you've no worries on that score. Now, are we going or do I have to thrown the tickets away."

"Oh, well...."

"That's settled then. I'll pick you up at seven o'clock and that will give us time for a quick drink in the Lion first. I'll bring Benny and his pyjamas and I'll call for Martha on the way." Des replaced the tickets in his wallet and Daphne knew the subject was closed. Her long delayed launch into village life was under-way.

   ***

Maureen came down from tucking Nita in and flopped into the armchair.

"All right, love?" Dan looked up from the paper he was reading.

"Worn out," she admitted. "Thank goodness that's over for another year."

"Aye," Dan nodded, "Happen next year she'll think herself too old for a party."

"We've been saying that for the last three years, and she'd still rather have a party than be taken to the cinema or something."

"Still, that magician was a rip-roaring success. That was a good move on your part. I've never seen a bunch of kids stay quiet for so long."

"No, you're right." Maureen smiled as she remembered the looks on the children's faces, and the 'oohs' and 'aahs' that had accompanied the production of the rabbit from the hat. All the children had seemed to enjoy the party, and Maureen had saved the magician for last, when the guests had used up some of their energy and would sit quietly. She needn't have worried; they'd all been as good as gold, so that when Dan had come in from work, he'd declared he must be at the wrong house.

Dan laid his paper down. "You've worked hard today, you sit there and I'll go and make us a nice cuppa."

Maureen smiled at him gratefully, and allowed herself to doze while Dan cluttered around in the kitchen.

"I suppose you'll want to go to this farewell party of the Davidson's?" Dan asked as he came back into the room carrying the biscuit barrel.

"Oh I think so, don't you?" Maureen looked at her husband and caught the look in his eye, "No, of course you don't. I forgot, you hate parties. All right then," she sighed, "We won't go."

"Don't be silly, love, of course we'll go. I daresay I'll find someone there to have a natter to while all you women go all silly and giggly in a corner."

Maureen smiled. She guessed that was just the way it would be and she was looking forward to it.

CHAPTER SIX

"I'm sure I don't know why we're bothering with this," Richard complained as he eyed the already prepared food in the kitchen.

"Because we're leaving a village in which there's some very nice people. It may happen that we want to come back here one day, and I'd like everyone to have good memories of us."

"I think the chances of us coming back here are highly unlikely. I've never been particularly attracted to the village, and don't say you have because I know better - and what have any of the villagers ever done for us, eh?"

"Maybe not for you," Ann retorted, "But that's because you never make the effort. It may surprise you to know that I have made some good friends here, friends that I'll be sorry to leave."

It did surprise Richard to know that his wife had friends in the village, he wondered when she ever met them. He began to realise how little he knew of his wife and found himself wondering what the future held for them.

"Anyway," he said, "You're clashing with the major production of the year. Everyone will be at the last night of 'Charley's Aunt'. Isn't there always some sort of last night party or something?"

"This isn't the West End," Ann said, "Everyone who's in the play will come straight here; the play finishes about ten and some will probably come in their costumes which should liven the place up a bit. Anyway," she went on, changing the subject, "I hope you've come out here to make yourself useful?"

"No, it's your party, you see to it all."

Ann put down the knife she was using to chop the salad as though she was frightened what she might do with it. "For goodness sake, Richard, pull yourself together and act like the executive you pretend to be. Stop being childish and grow up, and you can start by taking those cloths and covering the tables in the other room." She indicated a pile of linen and Richard, unused to her tone, found himself obeying.

Sue came downstairs and, seeing her father had been press-ganged into helping (she knew he would not have volunteered) decided it would be wasting time for her to try and avoid being forced into service and, without being asked for once, went and helped her Dad prepare the occasional tables that were dotted around the dining room.

Ann continued the preparation of the food in the kitchen, torn between worrying about what was going wrong between herself and Richard, and enjoying the rare moments of harmony as the family worked together. When she heard Sue and Richard chuckling together she began to think that maybe there was hope for the future after all - and it was certainly worth fighting for.

***

Benny and Leo were playing in Leo's room when Daphne and Des left the bungalow to go and see the play, and Martha was happily ensconced in an armchair by the fire, her ball of wool at her feet and her needles clicking nineteen to the dozen. She had promised to tell the boys a story before they went to bed but that would be an hour or so yet.

"Funny," said Daphne as they walked carefully along the frosted pavement, "In many ways Martha is a typical spinster, and yet she can wind the children of this village round her little finger."

"Yes, you're right. I gave up reading stories to Benny years ago - he said he was too old, and yet he'll sit spellbound listening to Martha. She's a wonderful woman. You know she spent most of her adult life looking after her parents?"

"I'd heard," Daphne nodded, "Was there never a man in her life?"

"I think there's been one or two," Des said, "But not for years now. She does tend to keep herself to herself, doesn't she? I mean look at tonight - half the village is going to be at this play or the party, and there's Martha, sitting in your home, so that we can go out and enjoy ourselves."

"Do you think she's lonely?"

Des thought for a moment.

"I doubt it. She's very friendly with that young Miles woman - what's her name... Belinda, that's it. And she doesn't have any shortage of visitors. She tends to be the village agony aunt, and loads of people take their troubles to her. She's a good listener. I suppose she has the time, or makes the time to care."

They reached the door of the Red Lion and Des held the door open.

"I meant to ask you," Daphne said, as she entered, "Wouldn't you have liked to have brought your lady-friend tonight instead of me?"

"Betty's going out with her family tonight," Des explained, "Her cousins who live in Scotland are staying with her for the week." He looked at Daphne sternly, "And don't go getting the idea I only asked you because Betty wasn't available, that's not the truth at all. I'm still treading carefully where Betty is concerned but I've told her all about you and she's looking forward to meeting you."

"You like her a lot, don't you?"

"Very much," Des admitted, "But I don't want to frighten her off by being too pushy."

"I'm sure you'll do just fine." Daphne smiled at him as she sat down at the table in the corner. She looked round the pub and recognised several people from the village. Hannah must have let Joe out tonight then, and there was Dan Evans - his wife seemed like a nice woman, she was always very friendly when Daphne encountered her in the village stores; Dan was talking to a man that Daphne recognised as being Dan's neighbour although she didn't know his name, and there was a couple at one of the other tables that Daphne didn't recognise. As she caught the woman's eye the woman smiled at her and Daphne returned the smile before turning her gaze to the glass that Des placed in front of her.

"Don't hold out much hope for that Miles woman tonight - her husband looks drunk already."

Daphne followed his gaze to the figure at the end of the bar. Harry Miles was an unpleasant sight at the best of times, Daphne thought, but tonight he was unshaven and dirty and obviously drunk, and Daphne was more than ever grateful that she wasn't Belinda Miles.

The couple Daphne had noticed had finished their drinks and got up and walked out, nodding at Daphne and Des as they passed.

"They're the people that are moving into the McDonald place," Des said. "I didn't know they had moved in already, but I suppose they must have." He looked at his watch, "I think it's time we weren't here."

Five minutes later they took their seats in the village hall. Daphne looked around and noticed many faces she knew. Well, this would set their tongues talking, seeing her and Des Palmer together. She smiled a secret smile, they were so wrong. She spotted the couple who had been in the pub and the man gave a little wave. Daphne gave a half-smile before turning her attention to the girl who had come for her order for an interval drink of tea or coffee and then she settled back to wait for the curtain to go up. The hall was alive with anticipation and excited chatter; she doubted there was a theatre anywhere in the West End that generated more excitement amongst its audience who, in their way, were as much a part of the performance as the players.

The play was performed with only minor hitches that just added to the charm and to the enjoyment of the audience. Daphne hadn't realised that Hannah Hughes was so accomplished an actress or that the village harboured so much talent. By the interval her sides were aching from laughing and, as the curtain fell she turned to Des, her eyes bright and shining.

"Oh, thank you, Des," she said, "Thank you for bringing me."

"Enjoying yourself, are you?" he asked unnecessarily.

"Des, I haven't laughed so much in years."

"Good. I knew it would do you good to come out."

Their coffee was brought to them and they sat sipping it. Several people came up and spoke to Des, people Daphne recognised as living in the village. Maureen Evans came up and said "Hello," including Daphne in the greeting.

"How are you enjoying the play?" she asked.

"Oh, very much," Daphne replied.

"That's good. Are you going round to the party afterwards?"

Daphne looked at Des. "What party?"

"The Davidsons leaving party," he explained, "Everyone's going round there after the performance. I meant to mention it earlier, but it slipped my mind. I thought we might join them. What do you think?"

"Oh, no. No, I don't think I'd like that at all." Daphne shuddered inwardly at the thought of confronting Richard Davidson. As far as she was concerned she never wanted to see that snake again. Her cup clattered as she replaced it in her saucer. Dan put out a steadying hand.

"It's okay, we don't have to go."

Daphne could see that Des thought that it was the idea of mixing with all those people that was putting her off the party and she let him go on thinking that, although, secretly, she was having such a good time she didn't want the evening to end.

"There'll be other parties," Maureen said. "Still, it's nice to see you here, Mrs. Taylor."

"Oh, call me Daphne, please," Daphne had recovered her composure now the danger was passed.

"Well then, Daphne, I hope to see you again. Meanwhile, I'd better get back to the kitchen. Would you like me to take your cups back?"

When Maureen had gone Daphne commented to Des on how nice she was.

"Most people are when you get to know them." He looked meaningfully at her, "But you have to make an effort to meet them half-way."

Daphne knew what he was getting at and, for the first time since living in the village, she found herself resolving to join in more with life in the community. After all, it would probably benefit Leo as well as herself.

***

The Davidson's party began well. Nearly everyone who was anyone in the village was there, with a few minor exceptions. Many of the guests had come straight from the village hall and the air of gaiety was still on them, so that laughter was never very far away. The music was loud, but confined to one room, so that those who wanted to talk rather than dance could sit in the dining room where the buffet was displayed.

Everyone admired the spread of food and congratulated Ann on the effort she must have put into the preparation. Ann was quick to ensure that Richard and Sue were given credit for their help.

"And where is Sue tonight?" asked Hannah. "I thought she'd put in an appearance."

"Oh, no," said Ann, "We thought it best to keep her right out of the way. She's spending the night with Nita Evans. Young Scarlett and her boyfriend are baby-sitting so that Maureen and Dan can be here." She nodded to the corner where Maureen and Ann were sitting with Tom and Helen Jermain.

"Nita's going to miss Sue, isn't she?" Hannah commented, "So's my Shirley, come to that."

"Well, I've told them both they'll be able to come and stay when we're settled. Sue tells me those people in the McDonald place have a daughter."

"That's right, Shirley did mention it. They were at the play, you know."

"Yes, I heard they were there. I didn't realise they'd actually moved in yet, otherwise I would have invited them to the party. It would have been a nice way for them to meet people."

"They're not living here yet," Richard said as he swapped his wife's empty glass for a fresh one. "I gather they're staying at a Hotel in Colchester so as to be close while the work's being finished off. I believe they're moving in next week."

"That's one of the perks of being married to a banker," Ann said to Hannah, "He can report on other people's affairs even if he can't tell me about his own."

Richard looked suitably shocked and Hannah thought his eyes held a momentary stab of fear.

"Don't go saying things like that, Ann, you could get me into trouble. You know very well that I never indulge in gossip or reveal things I learn about my clients."

Ann giggled and Hannah thought she was probably a little drunk.

"Don't be silly, dear," Ann said as she patted Richard's arm, spilling her drink in the process, "I was only joking."

"Well, jokes like that can backfire," Richard brushed his wife's hand away, "Don't let me hear you repeating anything like that again."

"Oh, all right," Ann said petulantly.

Richard shot his wife a seething glance before walking off.

"Well, I suppose I'd better circulate before I have too much of this..." Ann waved her glass in the air, "...and can't stand up." She giggled then leant forward and said conspiratorially, "Not that Richard takes any notice of me even if I'm lying down." She turned abruptly, spilling more of her drink as she did so, and headed off in the direction of the buffet. Hannah hoped she'd eat something that would help mop up the effects of the alcohol.

"Penny for them." Joe had come up behind Hannah.

"Oh, I don't know, I was just thinking of poor Ann and what's going to become of her."

"Well, this move could help them, you know," Joe said as he and Hannah walked towards the drinks table.

"I think Ann hopes it will," Hannah agreed, "But a new house doesn't necessarily mean a better life, they'll both have to work at it and I'm not sure that Richard will."

"Well, your worrying about them isn't going to help I'm afraid, so how do you fancy a dance - to cheer you up?"

Hannah flung off the cloak of despondency that was beginning to settle on her shoulders. Joe was right, it was pointless her worrying about things she could do nothing about. Gratefully, she smiled at her husband and, taking his hands, allowed herself to be led into a foxtrot.

John and Barbara Soames from Hill House were at the party and dancing the night away. Mary, who Barbara usually referred to as "Mother Mary" had been invited but had declared herself "too old for such frivolities" and was content to stay at home and listen to the wireless. "She seems to enjoy her own company more than ours," complained Barbara.

Maureen and Dan spent much of the evening chatting to Tom and Helen Jermain although all of them joined in some of the dancing.

Richard was acting as barman and nobody was allowed to have an empty glass for long. Ann was getting steadily more tipsy and endeavouring to steer clear of Richard's critical glance.

***

Belinda heard Harry as he tried to get his key in the lock of their front door. Her heart sunk; he was drunk again. She toyed with the idea of hurrying off to bed and pretending to be asleep but knew that it would make no difference, he'd just haul her out of bed and beat up on her anyway. She sat silently. Waiting.

The door burst open and Harry stood there. Sixteen stone of muscle. Dirty, unshaven, stomach flesh exposed, and she wondered what the Hell she saw in him.

"Well?" he demanded.

"Well, what?" Just as she expected he was aggressive. Occasionally, just occasionally, his drunkenness took a different turn and he would flop down on the settee and go to sleep. That way he slept off his aggression and was simply bad-tempered when he woke, but not violent.

"Well, why aren't we invited to this party, then?"

Belinda sighed. They *had* been invited actually. Ann Davidson had stopped her in the street a couple of days ago but Belinda hadn't told Harry. He would have wanted to go and that could have turned into a disaster. The combination of free alcohol, Harry and her just didn't mix and she made it a practice never to go anywhere with Harry where there was likely to be any alcohol at all. Consequently they never went anywhere together as Harry wouldn't go anywhere where there wasn't alcoholic drink available.

"I'll tell you why," Harry came and stood in front of her and, bending down, stuck his face on a level with hers, "It's because you're so bloody miserable, that's why. Nobody would want a wet blanket like you at a party, you'd kill it."

Belinda sat quietly, not daring to make a murmur, hoping that Harry would get bored and go away.

No such luck. He grabbed her arm and yanked her up out of the chair. "That's right, isn't it?" He was so close the spittle from his mouth sprayed her face and it took all her willpower to stop herself from rubbing it off.

She didn't see the fist coming, but she felt the pain as two teeth disconnected from her gum. She screamed and Harry hit her again. The punch to her stomach winded her and she bent double. Harry chopped the back of her neck and the floor rushed up to meet her.

***

"So when's your Scarlett getting married?" Helen asked Maureen as their husbands led them to a seat after a rather hectic polka.

"I think they've decided on the twentieth of November," Maureen said. "That way they think they'll be settled in by Christmas."

"I expect you'll miss her?"

Maureen, in fact, was trying not to think what life would be like without her elder daughter living at home. Lots of people told her that life would be a lot easier with one less person to look after but, in truth, Scarlett caused very little extra work. She did her own washing and ironing and often helped cook the meals and do the housework. Maureen would miss the chat, she wouldn't just be losing a daughter, and she'd be losing a friend as well. Much as she loved Nita, the younger girl's conversation level just wasn't adult enough to make chatter an interesting pastime.

She nodded now. "Yes, I'm sure I will," she said, "But they won't be far away and Eric has promised to bring her home every weekend to visit."

The conversation was halted as they caught sight of Ann Davidson heading in their direction. By now Ann was very drunk and she staggered rather than walked. Maureen was struck by a sudden stab of pity for this lonely woman. She got up, wanting to protect Ann from the stares of the guests but Ann pushed her guiding arm aside.

"Where's my husband?" she shouted. "He's gone off with that trollop, I bet. That brazen hussy dares to come to my party and steal my husband from me. He's with her, you can bet on it."

Maureen looked round the room. There was no sign of Richard and she realised she hadn't seen him for some time. She looked across at Dan and the years of closeness between them meant that he read her look exactly. He got up and left the room and Maureen knew he wouldn't come back until he found Richard.

"Why don't you come and sit down, Ann?" she said, turning back to the drunken woman. "We'll find Richard for you."

The rest of the guests had all gathered in the dining room now, drawn by Ann's shouting. They stood, unsure of what to do, the expressions on their faces ranging from embarrassment, through pity, to contempt.

"You'll find Richard?" Ann turned to Maureen and peered drunkenly at her, "You'll bring him back to me?"

"We will, Ann. Now come and sit here with Helen, while I go and help Dan find him."

"And that woman!" Ann's voice was raised again; "She'll be with him. Throw her out."

"I will," said Maureen soothingly. Ann sat down and rested her arms haphazardly on the table before dropping her head on them; her blonde hair flopping around her head.

Maureen hurried out of the room and through the hall wondering where Dan had gone. She heard a door shut somewhere upstairs and Dan's voice. "I don't care, Richard, she's your wife and your responsibility, and this is something you have to deal with."

Relieved that Richard had been found, Maureen stood and waited as he and Dan descended the stairs. Maureen didn't recognise the woman who followed them, but she noticed that the woman was still doing the buttons up on her blouse and Maureen was shocked. Surely Richard hadn't...no; he couldn't have done...not in his own home.

She stood aside to let Richard pass.

"Ann's in the dining room," Dan said to Richard. "Wait a couple of minutes then take her upstairs and put her to bed." He turned to the woman following him. "You've got two minutes to find your coat and be out of here. I think it's better if Ann doesn't catch sight of you."

The woman remained silent as she sorted through the coats on the peg and took a coat that looked suspiciously like mink from one of the pegs. Maureen wondered how such a young woman could afford such a coat then chided herself for the uncharitable answer that popped into her head. She and Dan watched the unwelcome guest depart without a word and Dan turned to his wife.

"I've told Richard to tell Ann he'd found the party too stuffy and had gone for a walk. It's best, I think."

Maureen nodded and took Dan's hand, glad that her husband was someone who she could rely on, confident that he could be trusted and thankful for the luck that had brought them together so many years ago. "I love you, Mr. Evans."

Dan put his arm round her. "Time to go home, I think, don't you?"

CHAPTER SEVEN

Daphne was woken the next morning by noises in the kitchen and she guessed that Benny and Leo were getting breakfast. The prospect did not thrill her with joy. She still had vivid memories of the previous occasion that Leo had decided to prepare her breakfast and she had been forced to eat three slices of burnt toast and a cup of lukewarm, milky tea.

When the knock on the bedroom door came she arranged her face in what she hoped was an expression of pleasant surprise before calling to the boys to come in.

Leo, a look of utmost concentration on his face, came first, carefully balancing the tray. Benny followed behind in an obviously supervisory capacity.

Daphne wrapped her bed-jacket round her shoulders before taking the tray from her son and she gave a mental sigh of relief at the sight on the tray. Two slices of toast, just the right shade of brown and dripping with butter, and a small jar of marmalade. A steaming hot cup of rich brown tea and a small spray of violets to complete the display.

"This looks lovely," she said truthfully. "Thanks, boys."

"Leo did it all, Mrs. Taylor, I only watched."

Yes, thought Daphne, and told him what to do, and mopped up after him I've no doubt.

"Well, it looks splendid," she said aloud. "What about you two, what are you having?"

"Ours is in the kitchen. Come on, Leo, before ours gets cold."

The two boys left Daphne to breakfast in peace and she wondered again as she did so, at the strangeness of the friendship between her son and Benny and at the quirks of fate that had brought into her life not only a friend for her son, but a friend for herself as well.

She had thoroughly enjoyed the previous evening's play and she knew she had Des to thank, not just for that but for restoring her self-esteem as well. The very fact that he obviously enjoyed her company, and the compliments he paid her served to repair the damage that Derek had done in the years of their marriage.

Suddenly it didn't seem as important whether or not other people knew she had a husband somewhere. She wasn't the first woman to be left and she was darn sure she wouldn't be the last. But, for the first time ever, she began to think that maybe the breakdown of her marriage hadn't been all her fault after all; maybe Derek could take some of the blame.

Des had invited her and Leo to Sunday dinner, saying it was about time they repaid some of her hospitality and she had arranged to drop the boys off on her way to church.

"Church?" Des had queried.

"Yes, Church." Daphne was definite. "It's time I started joining in things in this village, it will be better for Leo and better for me."

"Good for you." Des had gathered her up in his arms and hugged her - a hug from one friend to another, nothing more, and that was good too. It was good to have a friend, she wasn't ready yet for a lover and they both knew that if she ever was it wouldn't be Des.

When she got up she took the tray through to the kitchen and was amazed to see the boys washing up.

"Just leave the tray on the table, Mrs. Taylor," Benny said from his position at the sink, "We'll get to it later."

"Thank you, Benny. You're certainly very domesticated."

"Have to be, since Mum died."

Daphne could have bitten her tongue out; what a tactless thing for her to say. Fortunately Benny seemed unconcerned and had returned his attention to the washing up. Leo was concentrating hard on getting the plates perfectly dry, and Daphne tiptoed out of the kitchen before she could put her foot in it again.

Daphne walked briskly along the lane leading to the church. The rain that had fallen steadily through the week had meant that the footpath through the Churchyard was too muddy for her high-heel shoes whereas the lane, though unevenly surfaced, was fairly firm. Several cars drove past her and many hands were lifted in acknowledgement. She passed the Big House and wondered how the party had gone the night before and hoped that Richard Davidson would not choose this moment to walk out into his garden. Behind the Big House - part of the ground belonging to the house in fact - was the concrete area used by church visitors for parking their cars. There were none she recognised, but she reasoned that the few people she knew lived in the heart of the village and would not need wheels to get them to church.

She put her hand on the huge brass ring of the church door and hesitated. Could she go through with it? It had been one thing to take part in a village activity with Des' support, but venturing out on her own was a different thing entirely.

She took a deep breath and turned the ring.

"Good morning, Mrs. Taylor." Dan Evans beamed at her as he handed her the Prayer and Hymn book, "How nice to see you."

He seemed to mean what he said and Daphne felt a warm, comfortable glow spread over her.

"Maureen's down near the front," Dan went on, "Why don't you go and join her."

"Thank you, but I think I'll stay near the back today."

Dan nodded in an understanding fashion. "Well, there's biscuits and coffee in the Church Hall afterwards if you feel like a chat. I hope you enjoy the service." He smiled before turning away to pick up the next set of books.

Without making her feel embarrassed by taking too much interest in her, everyone was very friendly and nodded or spoke a greeting to her. Afterwards, it was with reluctance that she turned down the Reverend Watson's invitation to join the congregation in the Church Hall, explaining that she must get home to see what her son was up to.

"You must bring young Leo with you next time," he said. "He's a very special boy, and I'm sure he would enjoy Sunday School.

Daphne thought he probably would. Leo was naturally gregarious, which made life hard for him sometimes; it wasn't everyone who accepted easily those who were a little different to themselves.

***

Sunday at the Davidson's had been spent clearing up after the party and Richard had disappeared around lunchtime saying there were various people in the village he wanted to say goodbye to. Ann wondered why he hadn't said goodbye the night before, all his friends had surely been at the party, but she decided not to say point this out to him. It seemed wiser to keep quiet where Richard was concerned these days. She and Sue had made a start on the packing but Ann was becoming dismayed at how long everything took. They were to move out on Thursday and, if they continued at this rate, they would be nowhere near ready.

Richard came back at tea-time. There were no explanations as to where he had been and Ann maintained her silence on the subject. She was relieved to see he mucked in and, although they worked in silence, at least the family were working together.

Sue went off to bed at nine and Ann followed an hour later, declaring she was fit to drop. Richard said he'd carry on packing for a while and Ann went upstairs alone. When she awoke in the night she reached out and was alarmed to find Richard's side of the bed was empty. The clock said it was two-thirty in the morning. Surely Richard wasn't still packing? She listened for sounds but the house was quiet.

Wrapping her dressing-gown around her against the winter chill, she made her way downstairs and could see a beam of light spilling through the open kitchen door. Richard was sitting at the table, his hands wrapped round a mug of steaming coffee. He looked up as she entered.

"Got one of those for me?" Ann asked cheerfully, relieved that her voice didn't sound as worried as she felt.

"Sure." Richard got up and fetched the milk from the "fridge. "Sit down, Ann, I'll make it."

Ann watched her husband as he moved around the kitchen. He had seemed so distant lately, so far away from her. She still clung to the hope that this move might bring them closer together but she wondered if she were only fooling herself.

He put her coffee on the table and resumed his seat.

"Ann, there's something I ought to say...."

Scared, she put out her hand as if to ward off a blow.

"There's no need...." she began. She was frightened, but she wasn't sure what of. Revelations she didn't want to hear, she supposed.

"There's every need," he said. "The truth is, Ann, I've been a fool. I've done things only an idiot would do, and I've put our marriage and our happiness at risk." He looked up at her. "I love you, you know," he said softly, and she nodded, helpless, lost in the warmth of his eyes.

"Nothing I've done has touched the way I feel for you," he went on, "But I suddenly realised how I must look in the eyes of others - a grown up child who wants the whole sweet shop which would only make him sick anyway."

Ann didn't want to know anymore. She wondered what had happened to prompt this confession. Perhaps it was the forthcoming change in their lives, or had something happened at the party? She decided she really didn't want to know.

"It's all right, Richard. I love you too and together we'll be okay." Her throat tightened and she gulped, suddenly aware of how much she loved him. She knew she had been fooling herself for quite a while, trying to convince herself there was nothing really wrong between them. All the time there had been so much evidence that she had chosen to overlook, scared of losing him, of pushing him away with accusations.

He put out his hand and covered hers, which was resting on the table. "We'll be fine, won't we?"

She wasn't sure whether he was trying to convince himself or reassure her but she nodded anyway. She hesitated, she wasn't ready to give assurances that she didn't believe in.

How *did* she feel? Angry, for sure, but that anger was tempered by a kind of relief. Richard hadn't needed to go into details about what he'd been up to, she wasn't completely naïve, and hearing him admit it at least confirmed that her awful imaginings had been based in fact. But did she have no pride? Was she just going to let him off with a slapped wrist.

Yes, she decided, she was. If he meant what he said then bringing up the past would only add to the heartache. Put it behind them, that was the best thing.

"We'll be fine," she agreed. "I'm ready to go back to bed. How about you?"

"I'm ready." He stood up and put his arm round her and together they made their way upstairs.

***

The day after the Davidson's party Belinda had woken on the floor in the living room. Her body ached from the awkward position she had been laying in; her mouth hurt where her tooth was loose and where other teeth had cut the inside of her mouth and her ribs were tender. She wondered if they were broken as she tried to stand and felt pain cut through her.

With some difficulty she had crept up to the bedroom where Harry was asleep, sprawled uninvitingly across the bed. She crept back downstairs and there she stayed, nursing her pain and her heart-ache. Harry got up around tea-time and she heard him moving about, going into the kitchen - for a wash, she assumed and then back upstairs where there was the sound of drawers and doors banging. Eventually she heard him come down the stairs and leave the house by the front door. Suddenly she found she was breathing easier and she felt the muscles in her body which had been tense, relax. She went upstairs and changed the sheets on the bed, putting the old, vomit-stained ones into soak. Then she crawled into bed and fallen into a heavy, dreamless sleep.

Next morning she was up and out before Harry, who was asleep on the sofa in the front room, woke up. It crossed her mind to think that it was unusual behaviour for him to sleep on the sofa, which really wasn't large enough to accommodate his huge frame, rather than come and take over the bed, but the pain in her mouth was more acute this morning and pushed other thoughts swiftly from her mind. Her ribs, however, hurt less and she decided that she was probably not suffering from anything broken except her heart.

Belinda could tell that the dentist didn't believe her story of tripping up on the garden path and hitting her face on a stone flower pot. She'd been to see him too many times with similar problems for it to be true, but he extracted the loose tooth, and suggested that she try and take more care in the future.

Belinda knew what he was getting at - take care not to antagonise the attacker; but that was impossible. When Harry was drunk she only had to be there to annoy him and she couldn't see what she could do about it. Although.... Martha's idea of moving in with her was becoming more attractive by the minute. Okay, so they couldn't keep her presence there a secret, but at least she would be out of the house and out of the way of his fist. Besides, she had to face it, there was nowhere else for her to go. Maybe she'd go and have a chat with Martha when she got home.

Martha was delighted. Both to see her friend and at the idea of Belinda moving in.

They sat at the table, cups of tea in front of them.

"It will be lovely, my dear. You wait and see. It will be such fun to have some company. When are you going to bring your things across?"

Belinda thought of her 'things' and didn't think it would take long to collect them together. Although Harry had been generous to her at first with his gifts of gold and jewels, all of them had gone now, sold to support his drinking habit with the exception of her wedding ring which she had managed to keep him from getting his hands on. Apart from that there was very little in their house she valued. Anything she had liked - for instance the china dogs she had inherited from her parents, had been smashed in one or other of Harry's drunken rages.

"I don't know, Martha, I'll wait and see."

"Well, there's no time like the present. Why don't we go and collect your things now?"

Martha was worried that if Harry got his clutches into Belinda again she would change her mind about leaving. "Strike while the iron is hot" was Martha's motto, and she felt that the iron was at its hottest about now. If Belinda had time to think, she could cool off and lose the impetus to leave that brute of a husband of hers.

"I don't think now's a good time," Belinda said, "Harry's at home at the moment, It's best I wait until he's out."

Martha wasn't afraid of Harry - she'd nursed in the war and had faced fatal infectious diseases with the confidence that nothing could touch her, and she'd walked the streets during bombing raids, looking for the injured so she could help them and God had been with her. She was not about to be frightened by a bully, no matter how big he was. However, she knew that Belinda was frightened by him, and guessed that Harry grew powerful on his wife's fear, so she decided it would be best not to promote a further row.

"All right," she sighed, "We'll wait until you think the time is right." She leaned forward and laid a hand on her friend's arm. "Just remember, any time - day or night. All right?"

Belinda nodded. "All right, Martha," she laid her hand over the older woman's, "And thank you."

***

"Come on, Hannah, put your feet up." Joe pulled the armchair round in front of the fire and beckoned his wife. "I'll get the dinner, you sit here and rest. You look all in."

Hannah could hardly believe her ears. Joe get the dinner? That wasn't just unlikely - in her book it was impossible.

"Are you sure?"

"Just do as you are told and sit yourself down. He plumped up the cushion and Hannah had to admit to herself that the armchair did look inviting. Maybe just a few minutes....

She sank into the chair and gave into the tiredness that had been threatening to overcome her all day. The heat from the flames wrapped her in a warm cocoon and she closed her eyes. Just a few minutes, she thought, I'll just give my eyes a bit of a rest.

Within seconds sleep had overtaken her.

In the kitchen Joe pottered about, looking into cupboards and drawers, trying to find all the things he needed to cook a halfway decent meal. It had been a long while since he'd had to cook for himself. Not since before he and Hannah had got married, and that had been a few years ago now. What was it...eighteen, nineteen? Lord, Hannah would kill him if she knew he couldn't remember. Nineteen, that must be it, they'd been married eight years before Shirley was born, and she was eleven now. After her the babes had come thick and fast, but they'd all miscarried until Simon. Once he was born Joe and Hannah had decided that their family was complete. They were both in their late thirties by then and Joe didn't want to put Hannah through any more pregnancies. Nor did he want to see the sadness in her eyes when she lost a baby. It seemed that for a woman a baby was a baby as soon as it was conceived; whereas for him, at least, he couldn't think of it as a real person until that first moment he held it.

That was magic, pure magic. Holding a sweet little hand, counting ten tiny fingers as they curved round his finger. And watching Hannah feed the babes. The poet in Joe, usually well hidden, had wept at the pure beauty of seeing his wife, the mother, sustain her new-born children.

Now it pained him to see Hannah so tired all the time. He thought of other men's wives and how many of them didn't work at all, let alone put in all the hours under the sun as Hannah did. The shop opened six days a week at eight in the morning and didn't close until eight at night with the exception of Wednesday when it closed at two and Hannah went off to the W.I. Most of that time Hannah was behind the counter, slicing ham or weighing out sweets or cheese. If not she could be found in the garden collecting the eggs from the chickens or trying to catch up on the housework. Sundays she would cook the hams that the shop was noted for. Why, people came out from the town to buy their ham!

It wasn't right though, Joe thought. Hannah should have more time for herself, for working on the embroidery that she enjoyed, for being with the children and teaching them and reading to them or just for pleasing herself.

He made up his mind to go over the books that evening. Maybe, if they were careful, they could afford for Maureen to come in longer, or, if *she* couldn't manage it, maybe they could get someone else to come in a couple of afternoons a week.

Even when the shop was closed their lives were not their own. There would be people knocking on the door asking to be sold perhaps a bag of sugar or a quarter of a pound of butter. Hannah and Joe didn't really mind - the villagers were all their friends and if someone had run out of something they needed then what were shopkeepers for if not to serve their customers? It was just that there seemed no getting away from the business, never any let up.

A holiday! That was what was needed. A complete break from the shop. Why, that would do them all the world of good. If he was honest, he sometimes felt pretty worn out himself. Of course, they would have to get someone in to look after the shop, but that shouldn't be too much of a problem, there were one or two people in the village that he knew he could trust and who wouldn't mind taking over just for a week or two.

Suddenly excited at the prospect, he decided not to say anything to the family. He would draw some money out of their savings, and book a holiday to somewhere nice - Blackpool, perhaps, or Hastings, and it would be a lovely surprise for them. Yes, he thought, Hastings would be better, not so far to go.

CHAPTER EIGHT

Belinda really *had* meant to leave Harry. While she was sitting in Martha's kitchen on that Monday morning, the idea of not having to worry about listening for Harry's footsteps on the path or his key in the lock had seemed like bliss. Anything that would prevent another humiliating visit to the dentist where she would have to trot out the same, tired lies seemed like a Heaven sent solution. Then she realised that all it would mean was that she would be sitting in someone else's house listening for the same things that she listened for now. Moving across the road would only be a temporary respite.

Once home again she wondered how she could even have considered leaving. All her father's teachings came home to her. Marriage was a God-given gift he would say, and should be treasured and protected at all cost. Perhaps all marriages were not perfect, but difficulties were just tests set by God and should be worked at and overcome.

Belinda smiled wryly. Perhaps, before he died, her father should have had more words with Harry and Harry may have been different. But she doubted it. In her heart she doubted that her father had ever come across anyone like Harry or any marriage with the problems that she had.

She returned home to find Harry had gone out. Hopefully he had woken early enough to get himself off to work, he'd had too many days off lately for his own good and the last thing Belinda wanted was for Harry to get the sack. Not only would he take it out on her, somehow blaming her for it, but also she didn't want him at home 24 hours a day. At least the time he was working gave her a little peace.

She was restless that day. The little glimpse of a dream she'd had when she thought that moving to Martha's could be the answer had unsettled her. Ideas fought for superiority in her brain - maybe Harry, who obviously couldn't be happy with their marriage, would agree to her leaving, or maybe she and Martha could keep her presence at Martha's a secret, so that Harry wouldn't even know she was there.

These, and other thoughts that crowded in her head lasted but seconds. There seemed no solution out of this dilemma. Her father's teaching jostled with her thoughts of leaving and she knew she was trapped.

When Harry came in at half past six he was carrying a bunch of red roses which he handed to her silently.

Belinda was dumbstruck. He hadn't bought her flowers since their courting days. Perhaps he realised how close he'd been to losing her. She looked up at him. He was wearing his "I'm sorry, please forgive me," look and Belinda knew the forthcoming dialogue almost by heart.

She turned away from him and took a vase from the windowsill. When she felt his hand on her shoulder she froze. He turned her towards him, firmly but gently and she looked up at him.

"I'm sorry, Lindy, I know I shouldn't have hit you."

"No, you certainly shouldn't have." Belinda was surprised at the coolness of her tone. It would take more than a few red roses to get her forgiveness this time.

He crushed her to him, causing her to wince with pain as the bruised ribs took another battering.

"Forgive me, please. I'll never hit you again. I mean it, please believe me." His voice was breaking and a sob escaped from his mouth. Yes, things were following their normal pattern.

Belinda pushed herself from him and looked up into his eyes, where the usual tears were starting.

"Yes, I do believe you," she said, sadly. And she did. She was sure that when he made these promises he really believed he'd be able to keep them. It seemed that she knew him better than he knew himself. Perhaps the drink had addled his brain.

"So you forgive me?" He looked so hopeful standing there, like a little boy who'd been offered the possibility of an ice cream. Suddenly she felt his vulnerability and felt her power. At this moment she had the ability to hurt him. True, that hurt may erupt in temper that would be vented against her, but wasn't that because he loved her?

"Well..." she began.

He brushed his tears away and his eyes lit up. Correction, she thought, make that two ice creams and a soda pop thrown in.

"You promise? Never again?" Maybe the fact he'd bought her flowers proved something. Perhaps he was growing up at last.

"Never again." He pulled her back towards him and kissed her hungrily. She cried out in pain and he was immediately contrite.

"Oh, my poor baby." He stroked the outside of her mouth gently, then dropped kisses lightly on the place where she hurt. "I'll never hurt you again, sweetheart. Never."

He gathered her up in his strong arms and carried her upstairs. In the bedroom he laid her on the bed and gently covered her body with kisses as though trying to heal her wounds. Belinda wished that her heart could be healed as quickly as her body.

***

Everyone in the village found something nice to say about the party in the days that followed. They all agreed there had been plenty of good music. Most of the women said what a lovely spread of food there had been and hadn't Ann worked hard, while their husbands commented on the vast selection of drinks, both alcoholic and soft drinks. Nancy Dickens, who had always had a soft spot for Richard and who, some people suspected, had in her time been more than a friend to him, said wasn't it great to see that bitch, Ann, let her hair down for once, and Sam Elliot and Jim Warren wanted to know how Richard managed to get such a good looking piece of skirt into his bedroom and who was she, where did she come from and, more to the point, where did she go?

It hadn't taken long for tales of Richard's misdemeanour to get round the village and Maureen hoped that reports hadn't reached Ann before she left. It had been the talk of the Church Hall after morning service on the Sunday and Maureen had been glad that neither of the Davidsons were present. She guessed that Ann may not be feeling on top of the world, and both she and Richard were probably nursing a hangover. Besides which, it was only a few days until they moved and there was still an awful lot for them to do.

Maureen had hoped Ann would call in to say goodbye to her, but Ann was keeping a low profile and appeared to be staying indoors. Nobody had seen her since the party and Maureen guessed she was too embarrassed to face anyone. For this reason she decided against calling at the Big House to say farewell to her friend. Instead, she gave Nita a note to take with her when she went to see Sue on the day of the move.

The two girls managed to get in everyone's way as people hurried and scurried about or laboured under the weight of heavy furniture. Eventually they went and sat on the grass beneath the beech tree.

"You will write to me, won't you?" Nita asked for the seventh time that morning.

"Of course I will, but you've got to write back."

Nita nodded.

"And make sure the address on the envelopes is readable," Sue went on, "Or else I'll never get your letters."

Nita was hurt. "Don't worry, I'll get my Dad to write them."

"Good. And make sure Shirley writes as well and as soon as we're settled in you can both come and stay."

"What, both at once?"

"I don't see why not."

Their conversation was interrupted by Ann calling her daughter. "Come on, Sue, it's time to go."

The two girls hurried back to the house.

"Thank your Mum for her note, Nita," Ann said, "And tell her I'll write and give her our new address when we're settled in."

"Okay, Mrs. Davidson."

"Now, you two girls had better say goodbye, we're about to leave."

Sue and Nita looked at each other, both of them feeling a bit awkward and not sure what to do now the moment of parting had come.

"Out of the way, you two." Richard came out of the door carrying the family's budgerigar, Ricky.

"Well, at least you'll have someone to talk to on the way," Nita giggled as she nodded at the bird.

"Come along, Sue, time to get into the car." Ann put an arm round her daughter. She put her other arm round Nita.

"We're all going to miss you, young lady," she said, "You make sure you come and see us soon."

"I will."

Richard came over and smiled at the three of them.

"That's right," he said, "Don't forget, we're not at the other side of the world. We'll expect to see you soon." He turned to his wife. "Time we were off, love."

"Goodbye then, see you," said Nita and, with a final wave to her friend she set off down the drive and heard the car doors shutting behind her. She found her eyes were watering and she wasn't sure why. As the car swept passed her Richard tooted the horn and Sue turned and knelt on the back seat and waved until the car reached the main road and turned out of sight. It left Nita with a funny feeling to see her friend disappearing like that. She brushed her tears away as the big removal van trundled past her. She turned and looked back at the house.

It looked strange with all its windows black, without the softening effect of curtains, and Nita wondered whether the people who came to live there would have any children to play with. She was reminded of the people who were moving into the McDonald place, and wondered how old their daughter was. It would be interesting to have new people in the village.

"Do you think I will be able to go and see Sue?" Nita asked her mother later that day.

"Of course you will." Maureen gave her daughter a hug, aware that her daughter was experiencing some uncomfortable changes. "Probably not until the holidays, but I'm sure both you and Shirley will be invited."

Secretly Maureen thought that once Sue settled in at her new school and made some new friends she may well forget her promise to Nita and Shirley, but Maureen also knew that children of her younger daughter's age were very adaptable and it wouldn't be long before Nita forgot the promise as well. Maureen had been talking to Mr. Little, the new owner of the McDonald place, and had learnt that his daughter was only a few months younger than Nita. She hoped that her daughter would find a new friend in Caroline McDonald.

The McDonald place (was she ever going to learn to call it Yew Trees she wondered) was ready to move into and Mr. ('Call me Fred') Little, on one of his trips into the store, had announced the family's intention to move in during the Half-term holidays.

"Means my Caroline won't have to miss any school," he explained. "Not that she'd mind, of course," he gave a deep, throaty chuckle that made his whole plump body shake, "No doubt she'd rather have a couple of weeks off school."

Maureen nodded agreement, she was sure that Nita would jump at the chance of missing school as well.

"He seems like a nice chap," she had said to Dan that evening. "Very friendly."

"I hear he's quite wealthy," Dan commented. "The blokes in the pub were talking about him the other night. Apparently owns an engineering factory or something. What about his wife, what's she like?"

Maureen thought back to the slight, blonde-haired figure that had accompanied Fred Little. She had looked as though a puff of wind would blow her away and her hands and eyes had darted about the whole time she had been in the shop.

"I'm not sure," Maureen said in answer, "She seems not quite of this world, if you know what I mean."

Dan looked at her and nodded. "I think so."

"It's as though her body is here but her mind's somewhere else. She never actually said anything while she was in the shop, although she kept looking as if she was going to. Mind you, he seems to adore her."

Their talk was interrupted by the arrival home of Scarlett and Eric and discussions turned to the cottage that Scarlett and Eric were hoping to buy. 'Miller's End' needed quite a bit of decoration and the young couple were looking forward to it. They had plenty of time to decorate it nicely ('and it's much cheaper to do it ourselves' Eric had said) in time for the wedding.

***

Daphne had spent the Saturday morning shopping in town with Leo, and now they were home she was reviving herself with a welcome cup of coffee. She had kicked off her shoes and could feel herself gradually relaxing. Shopping in town was always stressful, and shopping with Leo was even more difficult. She loved her son, but his constant wish to browse through the westerns in the bookshop was very wearing. Now it was nice to be home and to put her feet up.

The knock on the door brought Leo running from his room where he had been reading.

"I'll get it, Mum," he said, and she smiled gratefully. A minute later he was back with Benny in tow.

"Dad sent a message," he said, holding out a piece of paper.

> *Dear Daphne,* Des had written in his bold, rounded hand, *I know this is really short notice, but June has agreed to come for a meal tonight. I was wondering if you and Leo would like to join us? She's dying to meet you and please don't think you will be intruding on an intimate candle-lit*

dinner - it was never intended to
be that, and anyway - I'm doing the
cooking! Please give Benny your
answer - and make it yes.

Des.

Daphne's first reaction was to refuse. Whatever Des said, she was sure he would rather be alone with his lady-friend than have outsiders present. Then she realised that he wouldn't be alone if Benny was there and at least with Leo there as well the two boys could keep one another occupied. Besides, it would be nice to eat a meal cooked by somebody else, and she was well aware that, whatever he said, Des was no slouch in the kitchen.

"Thank your Dad, Benny, "and tell him I look forward to it.

Benny"s face lit up. "You're coming to dinner," he told Leo, who gave a whoop of joy and started dancing round excitedly.

Benny turned his attention back to Daphne.

"Dad said if you said you said you were coming I'm to tell you dinner will be at seven o'clock."

"Thank you, Benny. I'll be there in good time."

"Well, I'd better get back, Mrs. Taylor. Dad wants to go shopping. See you later Leo."

Daphne stood at the window and watched Benny race off down the street, but she wasn't seeing him. She was wondering what on earth she was going to wear to a dinner party.

***

There had been a few occasions during the week when Nita had found herself missing Sue. Things would happen that normally she would run and tell her friend about, but now she was storing them carefully in her mind, ready to put down in a letter.

On the Saturday she decided to walk into the village and call for Shirley.

"Sorry," Shirley said sullenly, "Mum says I've got to stay in and help her."

"That's right," Hannah came through to the kitchen where the two girls were standing, "Shirley's got to stay in and tidy her room up this afternoon. She'll be able to come out tomorrow though."

Shirley scowled at her mother's departing back much to Nita's horror. She wouldn't dream of pulling faces at her mother even if she knew her mother wouldn't know. Besides which she never felt that her mother's demands on her time were really unreasonable.

"I'll call round in the morning then," she said. "About eleven. Okay?"

Shirley agreed it was all right and went off in a bad temper to obey her mother's instructions.

Outside the shop Nita bumped into Leo.

"Hello, Nita. Are you going somewhere nice?" Leo asked

"Not really. I was hoping to play with Shirley, but she can't come out today."

Leo sucked his thumb thoughtfully.

"My friend Benny has gone out with his Dad," he said, "So I haven't got anyone to play with either. I've got to be home by five, though, as we're going to dinner with Mr. Palmer," he said proudly. "If you could tell me when it's half past four we could go up to Hill House this afternoon."

"What? Just the two of us?"

"Less to get caught," Leo prompted.

Sometimes Leo actually made a lot of sense, Nita thought. With only two of them there would be less noise and therefore less possibility of anybody catching them.

She made her mind up.

"Okay. Come on then."

Together the two of them climbed the hill and took their usual route across the fields. Nita wished that she had worn boots, the earth was muddy after the recent rain and she could feel the mud squelching over the sides of her lace-ups and inside her shoes. Her Mum would kill her. Still, it was too late now, the damage was done.

When they reached the Hill House out-buildings they had a quick discussion and decided that they would both try and reach the house together; neither of them wanted to be the one who made the attempt alone. As usual, they had not formulated a plan for what to do in the event that they did reach the house, probably because Nita didn't expect to get that far without getting scared off and Leo just didn't think that far ahead.

Carefully, hand in hand, they tiptoed from the back of the shed, across the grass to the large tree that broke the line of hedging. From here lay the open area of lawn, which had to be covered before they reached the house.

Nita looked at Leo.

"Ready?" she asked.

Leo nodded and together they stepped out into the open.

There was no barking to warn them.

They were about ten feet away from the back door, when suddenly it was thrown open and a huge black creature came tearing out. Nita and Leo froze on the spot.

Oh, heck, thought Nita. Now we're done for.

"Keep quite still and he won't hurt you."

They looked up at the sound of the voice and saw a figure standing in the doorway.

"Oh no!" Leo cried, "The Witch."

CHAPTER NINE

"So you think I'm a witch, do you?" Mary asked as she placed the glasses of milk on the table.

"Well, no, not really." The girl, who said her name was Nita, was embarrassed, Mary could tell, but the boy she was with just stared. Mary suspected that the boy *did* think she was a witch - and found the possibility fascinating.

Once or twice previously Mary had seen a group of children from the village in the gardens of Hill House, and she had been disappointed that she had not been quick enough to catch them before. It had taken some persuasion to get Leo and Nita into the kitchen, but in the end they seemed less frightened of her than they were of Lucy, who seemed to imagine that they were sheep and she was a Border collie.

Once indoors she had told them her name in exchange for theirs, after which she put the biscuit tin on the table and both the children were tucking in to ginger nuts.

"It was a game," Nita said. "You being a witch was all part of a game."

"Ahh." Mary nodded, "And now I suppose the game is spoilt, now that you know I'm not a witch."

"Yes, I suppose it is really." The little girl looked crestfallen and Mary felt sorry for her. Then she was struck with an idea. She sat down at the table as well. "I'll tell you what, let's make a bargain. Why don't you tell your friends that you've met me and that I *am* a witch? That way you'll still be able to join in the game with them. And if you'd like to, you and Leo can come and play cards with me sometimes. It gets a bit lonely here all by myself."

"Do you live on your own?" Nita asked.

"Oh, no, dear. I live with my son. But you see he and his wife are out at work all day, so I have to amuse myself. As you can see -" she nodded at the walking stick that leant on the table, "- I can't walk very far, I can't even manage the walk down into the village, so I'm stuck here really. Now, would you like to come and play cards with me? Or snakes and ladders or lotto if you'd prefer."

The two children exchanged glances and Nita seemed to make a decision for the two of them.

"We'll have to ask our Mums," she said, "But if they say it's all right, we'll come up and see you lots. Won't we Leo?" She gave the boy, who was still staring open-mouthed at Mary, a nudge. At her prodding he nodded.

There was obviously something not quite right with the boy, Mary decided, but he seemed nice enough - and Lucy liked him. Once the children were seated at the table, Lucy had immediately sat beside Leo and rested her head on his knee.

"That's good." Mary leant back in her chair. "Now, as your parents don't know you're here this time I think you'd better get home now. Don't forget to let them know that you've been here, and tell them you're invited here again. If there's any problems they can always come and see me. All right?" She got up and, leaning heavily on her stick, made her way to the door.

At the door Nita shook Mary's hand and thanked her for the milk. What a polite little girl, Mary thought. Leo looked as though he would really like to shake her hand but didn't quite dare. He backed out the door, his dark eyes huge in his face, never taking his eyes off of her. Eventually, with a last glance back, he and the girl rounded the corner out on to the pavement and Mary returned to her loneliness. Strange how the house seemed even emptier now the children had gone, even though they'd been there for such a short while - but how much lighter her heart felt at the prospect of some young visitors.

While she didn't want to be ungrateful to her son and daughter-in-law they were not great company. By the time they'd had dinner all they wanted to do was watch television. Unfortunately, all Mary wanted to do was talk and sometimes she forgot herself and would start chatting during some apparently vital moment of a programme. This would result in an argument, which would end in Mary going to her room to listen to the wireless. Perhaps now the time spent in her room would be less boring, she could pretend the children were still with her or could plan things to do on their next visit.

***

Daphne spent ages sorting through her wardrobe looking for something suitable to wear to the dinner party. She wasn't sure how dressed up she was expected to be and her wardrobe was limited both because she'd had no cause to replace her out-of-fashion cocktail dresses and because funds were scarce and her small resources were mainly spent on food and minor luxuries. Clothes for herself were of secondary importance compared to things for Leo.

In the end she settled on a cream blouse with a long slim skirt and the usual high-heel shoes she wore to give herself some height. She tucked a black and cream silk scarf that she'd had for years in the neck of the blouse and pinned pearl earrings to her ears.

Leo was less problem and they were both ready in good time.

"Now remember, behave yourself," she said to her son as they walked the few hundred yards to Des's house.

"Aw, Mum," Leo complained good-naturedly.

"All right, all right. I know you're a good boy, but we don't know this June and we want her to like us, don't we?"

"Not half as much as Benny does," Leo said, "He's really worried about it."

"I expect he is," Daphne agreed, "But he's a nice boy, I'm sure June will like him."

Daphne liked June on sight.

The face that greeted her when the front door of Des's house was opened could never be called startlingly beautiful, but it was a face full of life with dark, sparkling eyes and dimpled rosy cheeks.

"You must be Daphne," she said as she stepped back into the hall and opened the door wider. "And you, young man, must be Leo. Come in, both of you. Des will be out in a minute, he's doing something wicked to some onions at the moment."

Daphne and Leo stepped into the hall and June held out her hands for their coats. "Silly really, me playing the hostess when you're probably more at home here than I am." She grinned at them. "I think Benny's in his bedroom," she said to Leo, "Why don't you run up and join him? Your Mum and I will be in the living room."

The two women watched Leo's departing back as he galloped up the stairs.

"Careful, now," Daphne called after him.

"He's not used to stairs," she explained as she turned back to the other woman, "And he's so clumsy, I always worry he'll miss his footing."

"Ah, well, he seems to have made it safely this time. Now, let's go in the living room, shall we? Des lit the fire in there and it's nice and warm.

Glad to get out of the chill hall, Daphne took a seat by the fire while June poured them both a sherry.

"I feel a fraud, doing this," she said, handing the glass to Daphne. "My first visit here and I'm waiting on you as if I own the place. But really, I'm just carrying out Des's orders."

"And doing it very well," Daphne smiled at her and then up at Des who entered the room rubbing his hands together.

"Being looked after then?" he asked.

"I certainly am. And I'm starving hungry, so I'm looking forward to dinner."

"Jolly good. Won't be long. I'll leave you two ladies to get acquainted then, shall I?"

"Go on, be off with you," June said good naturedly, "Go and slave over a hot stove while Daphne and I enjoy a good gossip."

She smiled at his departing back before turning her attention back to Daphne. "He's a nice guy," she said.

Daphne nodded.

"Yes, he certainly is. He's really done me a lot of good."

"Oh?" June looked curious.

"To cut a long story short, I was in serious danger of becoming a recluse, and if it hadn't been for Benny being friendly with Leo and thereby introducing me to Des, I'd still be sitting at home alone. Whereas, as you can see, I'm now out visiting like any normal person."

"Des did mention something about your having a secret past; it sounded very intriguing."

Suddenly Daphne found herself telling June all about Derek and her broken marriage and her fear of being found out in the village. It was as though she had been friends with the other woman for years instead of having only just met her.

"Oh, what a rough time you must have had," June said when Daphne had finished her story, "And being all alone to bring up Leo must have been very hard for you. Still, you've raised a boy to be proud of there, Des and Benny speak very highly of him."

"That's nice." Daphne couldn't help the little glow of pride that burned inside her. "Speaking of Benny, how have you been getting on with him?"

"Oh, fine. He was a bit quiet in the car when they picked me up, but once we got home here and he was able to show me his comics and talk to me about football he seemed to open up. He seems like a great boy."

"That's good. He was nervous of meeting you, you know."

"Really?" June looked thoughtful. "It's silly, isn't it. I was terrified of meeting him as well - and you and Leo."

Daphne was amazed. "Frightened of us. Whatever for?"

"Well, it's just that Des often thinks highly of you both, and I felt that I was sort of...on test. Oh, he never said anything of the sort, but I know he values your opinion."

"I'm quite sure there was never intended to be any sort of test," Daphne reassured the other women, "But if there was you would have passed anyway."

June opened her mouth to reply but was interrupted by the sound of a gong reverberating through the house.

"Come and get it."

The call was followed by the sound of Benny's door opening and two pairs of boys' boots as they careered down the stairs with loud whoops of joy.

The evening went well. The meal was superb and June seemed impressed; Daphne gathered that she had not had the pleasure of eating one of Des' meals before and had secretly not believed he could cook.

The meal over, Benny and Leo joined the adults for a game of snakes and ladders which Benny won, and then they went off to Benny's bedroom where they played, if not quietly then at least without too much noise. The adults played cards - gin rummy and knock out whist until nine-thirty when Daphne declared she was whacked and, anyway, it was time Leo was in bed.

As they said their goodbyes Daphne was touched when June leant forward and kissed her on the cheek.

"It's been great meeting you, Daphne - you and your good-looking son." She smiled at Leo who grinned and looked like the cat that'd got the cream, "I hope we see lots more of you."

Des moved closer to June and put his arm round her shoulders, "I'm sure we will, thanks for coming, Daphne - and you Leo."

"Thanks for the meal, it was wonderful." Daphne took her son by the hand and walked home thoughtfully, wondering at the way her life had changed. For years she had kept herself to herself in the village, scarcely talking to anyone, now she was on nodding acquaintance with the rest of the villagers, she had Des and Benny and June as friends, and she knew without a shadow of a doubt that she and June were going to be really good friends. She cuddled Leo to her suddenly and he looked up, an expression of puzzlement on his face. "We're so lucky, Leo, we're so lucky.

***

"Just get up to your room and stay there until you can be civil." Hannah watched as her daughter flounced from the room, slamming the door behind her.

"Now what?" Joe sounded tired as he came through to the kitchen.

Hannah looked at him, at the care lines that were engraved on his face and thought how old he looked suddenly. She supposed she must look the same; after all, there were only a few months between them in age.

She pulled a chair out from the table and sank slowly on to it.

"It's Shirley again," she said, blinking back tears, "I just don't know what to say to her anymore. She never does as she's told, and she's so rude."

"There, there," Joe came and put an arm round her shoulders and she leant back against him gratefully. "How would you like a nice cup of tea."

Hannah sighed. Dear Joe - that was his panacea for everything - a nice cup of tea.

"That would be lovely," she got up to fill the kettle up but Joe beckoned her down.

"I'll make it for you, you just sit there. And I've got a bit of a surprise for you."

"For me? It's not my birthday is it?" Hannah forgot about the ongoing problems with her daughter as her curiosity was piqued.

"No it's not your birthday and yes, the surprise is for you, but not just for you. It's a surprise for all of us."

Hannah felt her tiredness vanishing. She loved surprises but they were few and far between in their lives; nice ones, anyway.

"What is it? What is it?"

"Stop bouncing about like that, woman. You'll break the chair. I'll tell you in a moment."

She tried to contain her exasperation while she watched Joe pottering about with the cups. Oh, why was he so slow?

Eventually he put the cups on the table and took his normal seat next to her.

"Well?" she demanded.

"Oh, yes," said Joe as if he had forgotten all about the promised surprise. Hannah knew he hadn't, it was just his way of teasing her. He fumbled in his pocket and pulled out an envelope.

"There you are, read that."

Hannah pulled a letter out of the envelope and looked at the address. It wasn't one she knew; in fact she didn't know anybody in Southend-on-Sea, certainly not someone who lived at Blue Bells Guest House. She cast her eyes down to the signature: A. M. Dalton. No, that name didn't register with her. Suddenly her brain put two and two together and she stared at Joe, open-mouthed.

"Read the letter, woman, don't sit there gawping."

With her heart fluttering and her fingers trembling Hannah did as she was told and discovered that they were to go on holiday to Southend for the first week in April. Two rooms had been booked, one for her and Joe and one for Shirley and Simon.

Slowly she put the letter down on the table.

"Oh, Joe. I can't believe it."

"Well, you'd better, because it's true all right. I'm sorry we've got to wait a few weeks, but half term would have been too short notice and I really didn't want Shirley to miss any school, so I though the Easter holidays would do nicely."

"Oh, it would, Joe, it would. But what about money? How are we going to pay for it?"

"Now, you're not to worry about that," said Joe, with the air of a man who was used to looking after the family's finances. "We've got a bit put by and we can afford a week away. It may mean we have to wait a few more months before we can change the car, but that old banger outside will do us a while yet."

"Oh, Joe, are you sure?" Hannah knew the car was important to them. Joe used it to deliver the orders to their customers and so it was an integral part of their livelihood.

"Quite sure," Joe said firmly. "Anyway, I was having a word with Sam Elliot, and he recommended "Blue Bells". Said he took his family there last year and it was very good value for money. I had thought we might go to Hastings, but Southend's that bit nearer and, anyway, don't you have a cousin or something there? Thought you might like to visit her."

"That's right. Geraldine. Fancy you remembering that. I haven't seen her since...well, not since our wedding." Hannah looked at Joe, her heart spilling over with gratitude. "Oh, thank you Joe, thank you."

Joe looked embarrassed but she could tell he was pleased that *she* was pleased. "Why don't you go

155

and tell young Shirley," he said gruffly. "Maybe something to look forward to will cheer her up."

"Hmm, chance would be a fine thing, but I'll give it a try." As Hannah left the room she felt the lightness in her step and marvelled at what a difference something to look forward to made. Maybe it would cheer Shirley up after all.

***

"The chap who's moved into the Davidson's old place came in the shop today," Maureen looked over her shoulder from her place at the cooker to where Dan was washing his hands at the sink.

"Oh?" Dan was busy searching for the soap in the water. "What's he like then?"

"It's hard to say really." Maureen, content that none of the saucepans were about to boil dry, moved across the kitchen and took the towel from its hook behind the door. She held it out to Dan. "He's all right, I suppose, but he was a bit - I don't know - not unfriendly, exactly, but abrupt."

"Perhaps he's shy." Dan hung the towel up again.

"Possibly."

"Ah well, plenty of time. We'll have to wait and see how he turns out." Dan picked up the newspaper from the dresser and went and sat at the dining room table.

"While you're there, Dan, lay the knives and forks out, will you?" Maureen rummaged in the drawer and handed Dan the required cutlery. "Fred Little came in as well."

Dan looked puzzled, "Fred Little?"

"Yes, you remember. The family who has bought the McDonald place. Now there's a friendly fellow, if ever I met one. So polite as well. Says he can't wait to join in the village life. They're moving in next week."

"Hmm, not much for the likes of him here, I shouldn't think."

"Oh, I don't know." Maureen came and put the salt and pepper on the table, "I think he's just made for the amateur dramatics, and I know he likes a pint in the pub. I think he'll settle down all right. Don't know about his wife though."

"You'll have to take her to the W.I." Dan suggested.

"I'm not sure that it will be her kind of thing, actually. We'll have to see. Someone I *would* like to take out is that Belinda Miles."

"Isn't that the young girl who lives in the cottages by the war memorial? Married to Harry Miles?"

"Yes, that's her. Oh, Dan," Maureen sat down next to Dan at the table and put her hand over her husbands. "She's such a poor little thing, always looks so frail and fragile - and I'm sure he doesn't treat her well."

Dan had seen Harry Miles in the pub quite a bit. In fact, now he came to think of it, Harry Miles seemed always to be in the Lion. He'd got a bit belligerent once or twice with the barmaids and Dan and the other fellows had tried to calm him down. It had usually ended with Miles slamming out of the bar. Thinking about it now Dan could see that Miles' wife might suffer when he got home.

"Any proof of that?" he asked, "I mean have you seen any bruising or anything?"

"Only once," Maureen said, "And she said she'd had a fall, which could have been true, of course. Still, if he hits her, the bruises might be under her clothes. Anyway, I didn't necessarily mean he treats her badly physically; it's just that he's such a big, bad-tempered brute of a man and Belinda's such a dainty little thing. Sort of like a scared mouse."

Dan knew just what his wife meant. On the rare occasions that he'd seen Belinda he had thought what a delicate thing she was although, being more charitable, he would have likened her to a china doll.

"Isn't she friendly with...what's her name...you know, the woman who lives in the bungalow next to the memorial?"

"Oh, you mean Martha. Martha Skingsley I think her name is. Yes, I believe she does see a bit of her, they've been in the shop together now I think of it. Seems an unlikely pairing."

Their conversation was interrupted by the sound of the front door slamming. Maureen and Dan looked at each other.

"No need to ask who that is," Dan said.

"When will she learn to close a door properly?" Maureen asked exasperatedly.

Dan smiled at his wife. It was difficult for her, he knew. Her elder child had always been so well-behaved and good-mannered. Scarlett had never slammed a door, or ripped a dress, or got mud in her shoes, or brought home a bucket of worms, and Maureen was finding it difficult to cope with a daughter that did all that - and more. Oh, she loved her youngest child, Dan knew that, but her fuse was shorter where Nita was concerned.

Nita burst into the room like a hurricane.

"Guess what. The people who have bought the McDonald place are moving in next week.

Dan and Maureen exchanged smiles.

"Yes, we know, Princess. Your Mum saw Mr. Little in the shop today."

"Oh." Nita's face dropped before brightening again, "Yes, but did you know his daughter is 11? That's the same age as me."

"I think we know how old you are." Dan grinned at his daughter, "But won't it be fine for you to have a new friend?"

Nita's expression said she wasn't convinced.

"Supposing I don't like her?"

"Well, if you don't like her I suppose you needn't have much to do with her. But that's a daft way to think. There's no reason to suppose you'll be anything but best of friends." Dan folded up the newspaper, which he had given up trying to read and leant back and laid it on the nearby armchair.

"Come on, young lady," his wife said, "Just time for you to wash your hands before dinner." The two females went off into the kitchen and Dan sighed. Sometimes he wished for a bit more male company, someone he could chat to about football and greyhound racing and pigeons. Someone with a bit more go than that wet drip of a fellow young Scarlett was getting married to. Still, they seemed happy enough, that was the main thing, and he need never worry that Eric wouldn't look after Scarlett. He heard Maureen and Nita chatting in the kitchen and went through to help carry the plates in. As he stood in the doorway, looking at two of the three women in his life, he couldn't help but smile and offer up a secret word of thanks to his God for having sent him such a wonderful family.

CHAPTER TEN

Fred Little gave his wife, Josephine, a quick peck on the cheek. "Put the kettle on, will you, love?"

His wife turned from her seat at the table where she was carefully unwrapping her collection of frog figures and smiled up at him.

"It's ...er..." she looked around the room.

"I've unpacked it and it's on the counter in the kitchen. Buck up, there's a good lass, the lads are fair gasping." He hurried back outside where he continued to supervise the unloading of crates and furniture. He could scarcely wait to get everything in and organised.

Fred fell in love with Yew Trees as soon as he saw it. As far as he knew Josephine felt the same although, even after fifteen years of marriage, he often found it difficult to tell what she was feeling. Still, she seemed contented enough with the moving plans and had hummed under her breath while they travelled down - always a good sign.

It had cost him a fortune to do the old place up but he thought it was worth it. The house had been let go to rack and ruin, that was the trouble. It had obviously stood empty for years, apart from the mice that had left their mark in the form of droppings on the bare floorboards. The back door had been forced open at some time and cigarette ends and other, even less savoury objects, were evidence of human trespassers. Still, that was all a thing of the past. Now Yew Trees looked bright and fresh. The external paint-work was white, contrasting beautifully with the rich burnt umber colour of the bricks, and internally all the paint-work gleamed and the bright wallpapers gave the house a welcoming feel.

As he looked back at the house from the side of the removal van Fred gave a smile of satisfaction. Everything was turning out very well. Yes, very well indeed.

Several hours later he felt just as happy but quite exhausted.

"You sit down and have a rest," Josephine told him, "I'll just go and...er...make you a...," her voice trailed off and her hands waved about at her sides as she headed towards the kitchen.

"...a nice cup of tea," Fred finished off quietly as he allowed the softness of the armchair to envelop him in its welcoming cushioning comfort.

He was dozing when a knock on the door catapulted him back into wakefulness.

"I'll get it," he called as he hauled himself up.

"Hello, Mr. Little, I'm Hannah, Hannah Hughes." The woman from the village stores stood on the doorstep and he smiled at her in recognition. She was clutching a red and blue towel, which was round something obviously hot, judging from the steam sneaking out between the creases.

"I thought your wife might be too tired to cook, what with the moving and all, and I took the liberty of making a little extra stew. Perhaps you could make use of it?" She held the still steaming towel towards him.

"Why, how kind." Fred was touched. "Won't you come in?"

"No, no, not now, I'm sure you'd rather not have visitors just yet. Another time if I may."

"Of course." Fred started to unwrap the towel and discovered a red enamelled saucepan from which some extremely appetising smells were drifting.

"Just drop the saucepan back in the shop when you're passing." She turned to leave then looked back over her shoulder. "Welcome to the village and we hope you'll all be very happy here."

"I'm sure we will. And thank you." Fred turned back into the house, closing the door behind him. Josephine appeared in the hall.

"Mmm, something smells nice."

"No need for you to cook tonight, sweetheart. The lady from the village stores has kindly provided us with dinner. Get some plates and I'll open a bottle of wine." He followed her into the kitchen and rummaged through the drawer looking for the bottle opener.

"Just wait until tomorrow, when Caroline's here. She'll love it, don't you think?" He didn't expect an answer and wasn't surprised when he didn't get one. Josephine was busy measuring out the right amount of milk into the cups and he knew that she could only concentrate on one thing at a time. He smiled at her and thought of his daughter, spending the night with her grandparents. Yes, he was sure she would be happy here, and from what he had seen of the village children they seemed a nice enough crowd. She'd soon make friends.

He found the bottle opener and went across to his wife, putting a restraining hand on her arm. "Leave that, love, we'll have some wine."

She turned to him, putting her hand up to her mouth. "But I've poured-"

"Don't worry about that. Leave it and we'll use it later. Sit down and I'll dish up the dinner."

She sat obediently at the table while he scurried around getting cutlery and plates and glasses. As he poured the wine he bend down and pecked her on the cheek, saying as he did so, "I'll tell you what, love. I think we're going to be very happy here."

***

"I just can't believe it," Belinda told Martha as the two friends chatted over coffee. "He's being so nice to me."

"Hmm." Martha couldn't believe it, either. Either Belinda was lying to her, and Martha really couldn't believe she'd do that, or Harry *was* being nice to his wife - and that was out of character. To Martha's mind it was only the lull before the storm. There was no point in unsettling Belinda, though; who looked happier than Martha had seen her for a long while. She was beginning to lose that unhealthy pallor and at last there were some roses in the younger woman's cheeks.

"He took me out at the weekend," Belinda went on.

"Oh?" Martha was noncommittal; expecting to hear that Belinda had been taken to the Red Lion and then ignored while Harry got drunk.

"We went for a really long walk."

"Well, that was romantic." Martha couldn't keep the sarcasm from her voice as she pictured her friend traipsing across wet fields in nearly freezing temperatures. Just, she thought, because Harry Miles was too tight to spend any money and take his wife out properly.

"Well, I don't know about that," Belinda had apparently missed the sarcasm, "But it was really nice, Martha." She leaned forward as her enthusiasm grew, "We wrapped up really warm with scarves and gloves and Harry leant me his thick socks he uses when he goes fishing and we walked across the fields down to the river. There's all sorts of wild-life about you know, and my Harry knows all about it, especially the birds."

Martha could scarcely believe it. Belinda was talking about Harry as though he was the best thing since sliced bread. This was the man who beat her black and blue, who broke her teeth and bruised her face and cracked her ribs. How could she possibly forgive that kind of treatment and give herself so willingly to such a brute of a man?

Martha sighed as she picked up the cups and went and ran them under the tap. "Another cup?" she asked.

Belinda nodded absently, a faraway look in her eye. "When we got home I needed help to get my boots off," she looked across at Martha, "You know what boots are like. Anyway, he took my boots and socks off and got some cream and massaged my feet. It was absolutely heaven. And then..." she blushed and her voice faltered, " Well, that was it really."

Martha poured out the fresh coffee and took it across to the table. "Well, I'm really glad things are going so well for you. But don't forget, will you -" she put her hand gently on the other woman's shoulder, "If anything should go wrong - and I'm not saying it will, mind; but if it should, then you come straight over here to me."

Belinda smiled, "Oh, it won't, Martha, it won't. Not now. All the bad times are behind us and ahead there's only joy." She looked so trusting and full of faith that Martha was astonished. She wouldn't have believed that anyone could be so naive.

As she took her seat at the table opposite her friend Martha found herself putting two and two together. There was a new spring in Belinda's step, a new glow in her face. The truth began to dawn on her.

"You're not..." she began but found herself unable to form the words.

"Expecting a baby?" Belinda finished for her in her soft voice. "Yes, Martha, I think I am. Harry's taking me to the Doctor's tonight, but I've...well, you know, I've missed a couple of months."

"Oh, my God." Martha felt the colour drain from her face as various implications occurred to her. Not only would Belinda be at risk from that brute of a man, she would be providing him with an innocent little soul for him to vent his anger on.

"Aren't you happy for me?" Belinda leant forward, obviously anxious for approval and congratulations.

Martha couldn't bring herself to say the words she knew her friend wanted to hear.

"I just hope you're doing the right thing, that's all."

"I don't know what you mean."

Martha felt her temper rising. "Oh, come on, Belinda, you're a big girl now, you don't need me to spell it out for you. That man you're married to has treated you like dirt ever since you've been wed. He thinks nothing of a well-aimed boot up your backside if you upset him and, let's face it, that's the least of the punishments he's handed out to you. How do you think a poor little nipper's going to fare when he upsets his Dad?"

Belinda stood up, her eyes blazing.

"My Harry wouldn't harm a little child, how dare you say such a thing? Okay, so he might have hit me a few times, but I deserved it. I'm being good now, so Harry doesn't need to hit me anymore and, anyway, he's got control of his temper. You may have helped me out once or twice, but that doesn't give you any right to say such awful things about my Harry."

Without another word Belinda took her coat from the back of the chair and stormed out of the house leaving Martha sitting at the table, bemused.

This time I've done it, Martha thought, this time I've really gone too far. She stood up and walked across and poured the untouched coffee down the sink. Out of the window she could see Belinda hurrying across the road and back to her house. Maybe Belinda didn't think Martha had the right to express her opinions, but Martha thought that being a friend gave her every right to warn Belinda, surely that's what friends were for. She watched as Belinda unlocked her front door and was swallowed up into the dark interior of her home and Martha offered up a small prayer for her friend's safety.

***

"He was a lot friendlier than the other one," said Hannah when she returned from delivering the stew to Fred Little. For once there were no customers in the shop and Joe was busy behind the counter reading a newspaper. He looked up when his wife came in.

"Everything all right then, Dear?" he asked.

"Yes, he seemed quite pleased."

"And so he should be. You women are a great lot," he said as he pulled down a jar of toffees and helped himself to one, "You really go out of your way to make newcomers feel welcome to the village. I suppose before the day is out there'll be a procession of women traipsing up the lane with various gifts. And all in the name of neighbourliness." He winked at her and added slyly, "Or is it just for the chance of having a nosy round, eh?"

"Joe Hughes, you should be ashamed of yourself. Why, I never even stepped inside the house when I was invited to."

"Ah well, happen you're different. I knew you were a bit special when I married you. But don't tell me that some of them other women don't only do the Good Samaritan bit so they can black their noses."

Hannah said nothing. She knew it was true, at least partly, that some of the women *did* like to give newcomers the 'once over' but it wasn't just that. The village of West Morling was a close-knit community. Everyone was on at least nodding acquaintance with everybody else and Hannah liked it that way. She had lived all her life in small villages and on her rare visits to large towns or cities found herself almost frightened of the crowds and hustle and bustle. Consequently, when new people moved into the village Hannah was happy to do something that she hoped would make them feel welcome. The women of the village all discussed in advance what each one would take so there would be no duplicating of gifts. One would take a meal, as Hannah had today; another would offer a cake or biscuits. Some would take bread or milk or cans of fruit while another might turn up with a flask of tea or some sandwiches.

Poor Sally Mailer had been the first to visit the new owner of the Big House. She had been the one with the tea and sandwiches and she had gone as soon as she had seen the removal van drive through the village. She reported that Mr. Barrett had looked down his nose at her and told her in no uncertain terms that he was perfectly capable of providing his own food and drink, thank you very much, at which she had retreated, hurt, with her metaphorical tail between her legs. She had then proceeded to warn the other members of the welcoming committee before they ran into the same treatment. Joe had declared himself quite happy with the outcome as the fruit cake that Hannah had prepared had been far too good to offer a stranger.

"I see you've been busy," Hannah said now, nodding at the newspaper. Joe jumped up and stood to attention. "Yes, missus, I have. Honest, guv. Why, I've served at least ten people since you've been gone and packed two orders ready for delivery." He gave a mock salute.

Hannah laughed at him, "Go on with you, you silly old fool. Best get those deliveries done then. I'll put the kettle on while you're out and we can have lunch when you get back."

"Okey, dokey. Won't be long then." Hannah watched from behind the counter as Joe put the two cardboard boxes laden with goods into the car and smiled at him as he doffed an imaginary cap before driving off. There was no doubt about it, he was a fool and she wouldn't have it any other way. The idea of the forthcoming holiday had done wonders for his general well-being, the lightness was back in his step and the smile came to his face more readily. She had to admit that she, too, was looking forward to the break.

She was in the kitchen putting the kettle on the hotplate when she heard the shop doorbell ring and she hurried through to greet her customer. She was not prepared for the sight that met her. Shirley stood in the middle of the shop with her arm round Nita who seemed to be covered with blood.

"Why, Nita, whatever's the matter?" Hannah's heart lurched. The girl lifted a face on which dirt and tears battled for supremacy.

"She fell over," Shirley spoke for her friend. "We was only playing," she added defensively.

"Let's have a look." Hannah lifted up the counter for the girls. "Out in the kitchen with the pair of you, I can't have you bleeding all over my shop now can I?" She patted Nita on the head. Nita continued to sob silently.

Hannah hurried after the girls and pulled out a chair for Nita to sit on. As the girl held out her hand Hannah gasped. Blood was pouring from her wrist and Hannah could see diamond-sparkles of glass protruding from the wound. She knew very little about first aid and had never been called upon to deal with anything more than the odd graze or two, but felt, instinctively, that here was something potentially dangerous. Didn't people kill themselves by cutting their wrists? She wondered how the injury had happened but decided now was not the moment to ask, time was too precious. Oh, God, what was she to do? She wished Joe were here, he'd know the best course of action.

Stop the bleeding. Yes, that was it. But she couldn't press down on the wound, could she? She'd only succeed in pressing the glass further in.

Wash it. She'd have to wash it to get the glass out.

"Shirley, run and tell Nita's Mum what's happened, will you?" She heard Shirley's intake of breath and guessed a complaint was coming. "No arguing, now. Oh, and on the way out, turn the sign on the shop round, will you? I don't want any customers for a few minutes."

She heard the shop door close behind her daughter as she filled a basin with cold water from the tap. "On second thoughts," she said, turning back to the injured girl, "You'd better come over here and we'll run the tap over the cut. That should get rid of some of the glass. Come along." She held her arm out and Nita crossed the kitchen, sniffing. With her good hand the girl wiped away tears, leaving another smudge of dirt as she did so.

"We were only playing," she said as she held her wrist out, echoing her friend's words.

"What were you doing then?" Hannah pulled Nita's wrist gently under the running tap, twisting it sideways so that the water ran across, rather than into the wound.

Nita started sobbing again.

"We were only pretending to be horses," she explained through her sobs, "but then I tripped, and I fell on some broken glass. Look," she held out her leg for inspection, "My leg's cut as well."

Hannah looked down and saw the superficial wound on the girl's leg, which was already forming a scab.

"I don't think we need worry about that now," she said. "Right, let's have a look at this." She drew the wrist towards her and brushed aside the two small pieces of glass she could still see and then, satisfied the cut was as clean as she could make it she grabbed a towel from the counter and held it over the wound. Nita caught her breath and Hannah realised she had probably hurt her.

"I'm sorry, Nita, but we must try and stop the bleeding. Do you think you can be a brave girl and hold that very tightly for me?"

Nita put her hand over the towel without answering.

"That's right," Hannah said gently, "Hold it as tight as you can-" The sound of the shop bell interrupted her. "Now who can that be? I told Shirley to put the closed sign up." Suddenly there was the sound of crying from upstairs and she realised that Simon had woken from his afternoon sleep. She felt the panic rise within her and forced herself to be calm.

"Sit tight a minute, Nita, I'll just see who that is in the shop."

She ran down the hall and through the living room and was relieved to see Daphne Taylor and her son.

"Oh, Daphne, just the person I could do with."

"I'm sorry," the other women said, "I didn't know if you were closed or not, but Leo ran on in and I just followed when I realised the door wasn't locked."

"That's all right. Look, would you mind coming through to the kitchen. Young Nita Evans has fallen over and hurt herself and I don't know what to do."

Daphne hurried round the counter, Leo in tow, and they followed as Hannah led the way. When they reached the hall Daphne tapped Hannah on the shoulder "Why don't you pop up and see to your little one? I'll see to Nita."

Hannah felt relief flood over her and she smiled gratefully. She wasn't used to having to deal with this kind of emergency and now she felt she could hand the responsibility to someone more capable.

She pointed towards the kitchen. "Nita's in there. Shirley's gone to get Nita's Mum but it'll be twenty minutes or so before they get back." She turned and hurried up to the stairs towards her crying son. Tears of a toddler who was only crying because he was hungry was something she *could* deal with.

CHAPTER ELEVEN

"Hello, Nita," Daphne was carefully cheerful as she greeted the pale child sitting in Hannah's kitchen. "Let's have a look at what you've been doing to yourself then."

Carefully she lifted the towel and saw that the wound was still bleeding freely.

"Right. Well, I think it might be an idea to pop you down the hospital and let the doctors have a look at that. All right?" She looked down at the girl who nodded.

"Leo," Daphne said, "You stay here and keep Nita occupied while I go and find someone with a car."

She hurried out of the room and called up to Hannah. "I need a car, Hannah. Where's Joe?"

Hannah appeared at the top of the stairs, her son on her hip. "He's out delivering," she said apologetically. "He'll be a while yet, he's going to old Mrs. Elliot, and he always stops and has a cuppa with her, says she's glad of the company."

"Well who else round here has got one, can you think of anyone? Anyone at all?"

Hannah looked thoughtful. "Well, there's Sam Elliot, but he's at work. Richard Davidson used to have one, of course, but he's gone."

Daphne felt exasperated. She couldn't think of anyone either. The families she knew of that owned a vehicle would have used it to get to work in.

"I know," she said suddenly. "What about the man whose moved into the Davidson's old house. He might have a car."

Hannah looked doubtful. "Well, he might, but I don't know that he'd lend it to you."

"I don't want to borrow it," Daphne said impatiently. "We need a driver, that's all. Someone to run us to hospital." She was already out of the door. "Leo's in the kitchen with Nita, I'll be back in a minute."

She hurried across the road and up the lane to the Big House. She pushed the bell but when she heard no corresponding ringing she knocked impatiently at the huge door-knocker.

"All right, all right, I'm coming." The voice was strong and deep and authoritative.

When the door opened Daphne's first thought was that she had never in her life seen such a good-looking man. For a few seconds all thoughts of Nita were wiped from her mind.

"Well?"

Her mind flew back to the present.

"Do you have a car?" She asked simply.

"I do. Who wants to know, and why?"

"Look, I know this is an awful cheek, but I wonder if you could possibly run us to the hospital in town. There's a young girl at the village store who has cut her wrist, and I think it will need stitches. I have no transport and we need someone to drive her in."

"I'm very sorry, Miss...er?" He raised one eyebrow quizzically.

"Taylor. Mrs. Taylor."

"Well, Mrs. Taylor. I'm very sorry, but I really am extremely busy. I simply can't spare the time to drive careless young girls around. Good afternoon."

He obviously intended to shut the door on her and Daphne found her temper rising. She put her hand on the door, preventing him closing it any further without it being awkward for him.

"Look, Mr. Barrett, I don't think you realise the seriousness of the situation. The girl in question is only eleven years old and she has had a bad fall, which could be extremely serious. I think it would be wise to get her to hospital as quickly as humanly possible. In this village we all help one another and I suggest if you intend to live here for any period of time you start showing you're a human being with feelings."

He looked at her in stony silence for a period of time; his blue eyes boring into her like a drill into a tooth. Abruptly, he turned and took a coat from the hall-stand.

"Come with me," he ordered and Daphne followed him obediently to the rear of the house where his car stood, gleaming and polished.

"Get in." He nodded at the passenger door and Daphne obeyed, reasoning that now was not the time to tell this arrogant man that she objected to being bossed about.

They drove in silence to the shop where Hannah was waiting anxiously.

"Will you be picking up Nita's mother on the way?" Hannah asked.

"No." Daphne was firm. She got out of the car and stood on the pavement. "I don't think there's time. Perhaps when Mr. Barrett gets back from taking us to the hospital he'll bring Maureen in." She smiled disarmingly at him and he scowled back.

"I'll go and get Nita." Hannah departed and Daphne turned and leaned through the car window.

"I know you're not very happy about doing this, but we will have a young, frightened girl with us in a minute. For goodness sake try and be nice for her sake."

He slammed his hands against the steering wheel.

"Now listen, young lady, I came to this village for peace and quiet. I expected to have to talk to nobody except maybe the delivery man and the milk man unless I chose to. Now here I find myself being chauffeur for the village and being expected to give up my time for all and sundry. It's too much, it really is."

"Sssh, here she comes." Daphne opened the car door. "Here you are, Nita, you sit in the front with Mr. Barrett." She helped the girl into the car and checked the towel was still in place.

"Don't worry about Leo," Hannah said, "I'll keep him here until you get back from the hospital."

"Oh, thank you, Hannah, that's kind of you. I'll be back as soon as I can."

Daphne got into the back of the car which drove off almost before she had a chance to close the door.

"Mr. Barrett lives in the Big House, Nita," she said, leaning forward in her seat. "Isn't it nice of him to take us to the hospital in his nice car?"

Nita turned a tear-stained face towards the man and stared at him solemnly. Daphne had to smile to herself when she saw the grimace on his face that he obviously thought of as a smile. At least he's trying, she thought.

In no time at all they pulled into the hospital grounds and Ken Barrett drove right up to the door.

"This do you?" he mumbled ungraciously.

"Thank you so much," Daphne said, putting on her sweetest smile. "Now don't forget you promised to go and collect Nita's mother. Please hurry, she must be frantic with worry."

"I never promised any such thing-" he began, but Daphne slammed the door on his astonished face and hurried Nita into the hospital reception area.

***

"I do hope she'll be all right," Hannah said as the family sat down to lunch. It was two-thirty in the afternoon and much later than usual for them to eat what should have been their mid-day meal, but Joe had been understanding and had praised Hannah for the way she had handled the situation with Nita.

"You did all the right things," he reassured her when she had bemoaned her lack of expertise, "And Nita's in good hands now."

"I still wish you had been here, Joe. At least you could have taken Nita to the hospital instead of that bad-tempered old man. Thank goodness you were here in time to take Maureen. The state she was in she wouldn't have wanted Mr. Barrett having a go at her."

"What did he say, exactly?"

"Well, he didn't really say anything when he was here, but Daphne Taylor said he was really rude to her. And you know how he was when he came back to get Maureen."

Joe smiled grimly. "I do indeed. I have to admit that he does have the personality of a wart hog. Still, it seems as though he wants to keep himself to himself which may be a good thing."

The shop bell rang and Hannah got up. "I'll go, I've finished." She put her plate in the sink as she passed on her way into the shop.

"Why, hello, Leo. Hello, Daphne. What can I do for you?"

"Hello, again. Do you know, in all the fuss with Nita, I clean forgot to get the loaf of bread I came in for in the first place. It wasn't until Leo asked for a sandwich that I realised." She took the loaf from Hannah and handed over the money. "So what did Ken Barrett say after I left? I didn't like to hang around and listen.

"Oh, he was quite rude I thought. As you know, Joe was back by then and he was going to run Maureen down to the hospital. In view of the fact that he apparently didn't take kindly to being troubled in the first place I would have thought that Mr. Barrett would have been pleased to not have to take Maureen. Instead he muttered about how he'd been mucked about and that people around here didn't seem to know quite what they were doing. He was still muttering when he got back in his car and drove off."

"I wondered if I ought to pop over and thank him for taking us," Daphne suggested.

Hannah was horrified. "Oh, no, I don't think that's a good idea at all. He doesn't seem too keen on visitors anyway, do you think?"

"No, I suppose not." Daphne looked disappointed and Hannah was surprised. She couldn't imagine that anyone would willingly lay themselves open to the sort of treatment that Ken Barrett seemed capable of handing out.

"Anyway," she went on, "I expect Maureen and Dan will go round and thank him when they get home from the hospital."

"Dan knows then?"

"Oh yes. Joe and Maureen called up at the farm on their way to the hospital and he went with them. He's at the hospital now."

"That's good."

"I think Dan wants a word with our friend at the Big House anyway," Hannah said, remembering a conversation she'd had with Maureen earlier in the week.

"Oh?"

"Yes. It seems that he's fenced off the piece of ground at the back of the Big House that the Church uses as a car park.

"He can't do that, surely?"

"Well, yes, he can actually. Its really his land but the Church has used it for years and years - certainly all the time the Davidson family have owned it. Now he's moved in and started throwing his weight around as if he owns the place." Hannah realised what she'd said and giggled.

"Oh, well, if he owns it..." said Daphne.

"That's not the point, though, is it? He must know he's upsetting people. If he's going to live in the village then I think he should take the rest of us into consideration."

Daphne smiled as she remembered her almost identical words to Ken Barrett just a few hours ago.

"You're probably right," she said. "It would have been better if he'd at least warned people what he was intending to do. Still, as we said, it *is* his land and he can do what he wants with it I suppose. Okay, then Leo, ready to go?" Ushering her son in front of her she said goodbye to Hannah. "Perhaps if you hear anything from the hospital you could let me know?"

Hannah nodded. "Of course. You do think she'll be all right, though?"

"I'm sure she will," Daphne said truthfully and she took Leo's hand. "Come on then, young man, let's go and make you this sandwich.

When they got home Daphne and Leo sat and ate their sandwiches by the roaring open fire and Daphne was rather surprised when Leo declared he was going out. It was a particularly cold day and she knew how much Leo enjoyed sitting by the fire curled up on the floor with one of his favourite westerns to read.

"Where are you going? Nita won't be able to come out and play, even if she's home from hospital, which I doubt, I expect they'll keep her in overnight."

"That's okay, I'll see who else is around."

"All right then. Be careful."

Daphne washed up the cups and saucers and plates and cleared up the mess Leo had left on the kitchen table where he'd been painting a picture of The Lone Ranger which was only recognisable as that character by the obvious mask he wore. Never mind, she thought, it keeps him happy. He'd been out playing with Benny all week but Benny and his Dad had gone to June's for dinner today and she wondered what children Leo would find to play with this afternoon.

Sitting back in her armchair by the fire she found herself thinking about Ken Barrett. It was true his manner had been extremely sullen and rude and yet she instinctively felt that beneath the harsh exterior lurked quite a pleasant man. She hoped she wasn't fooled into believing that because she found him so attractive, but she didn't think so. She was reminded of herself, how aloof she'd been from the village for so many years. All right, so she hadn't been downright rude, but she hadn't been particularly friendly either. Still, this business about the Church car parking didn't put him in a very good light. On the other hand, if it was his ground then he was perfectly within his rights.

A knock on the door disturbed her thoughts and she was surprised to find Dan Evans on the step.

"Hello, Dan, won't you come in?"

"No, I won't, Mrs. Taylor, if you don't mind. I'm just on my way home to pick up some bits and pieces for Nita but I wanted to call and say thank you."

"Oh, good Lord, that's all right. I didn't do anything. Hannah had done all the important things by the time I go there. How is Nita?"

"Oh, not too bad. She's cut a vein but thanks to Hannah's care she hadn't lost too much blood. She'll be in hospital for a day or two, but she's in no real danger."

"Oh, thank goodness. Give her my love, won't you. Tell her we look forward to seeing her back in the village."

"I will. And thank you again for everything you did. It helped her just having you there. Now I must be off, I'd better pop in and say my bit to Hannah and then I suppose I'd better call at Mr. Barrett's place."

"Confront the lion in his den, is that it?"

"Oh, surely he's not that bad? All I hear is bad reports of the man and yet he is one of the reasons my Nita got to hospital on time."

"Well, he didn't exactly do it with good grace," said Daphne, "But I suppose he did do it, and that's all that matters in the end I guess."

Dan nodded his agreement and, with a wave of his hand, left Daphne to return to her armchair and her thoughts which, she was surprised to note, in no time at all had returned to Ken Barrett; to his piercing blue eyes and determined jaw and a grimace that passed for a smile. She found herself wishing, despite all the appearances the man gave of being a totally unlikeable person, that she could get to know him better.

***

Leo panted as he climbed up the steep hill.

He was vaguely aware that if he had taken time to think about it, he wouldn't be doing this at all. Secretly he still believed the lady called Mary was a witch. A nice witches maybe, but still a witch.

Still, somehow Leo guessed that Mary would want to know what had happened to Nita and, as he had been there for most of it, he felt it was up to him to tell her.

He went to the front door of Hill House this time; no sneaking in at the back for him anymore - he was on Official Business with capital letters and he drew himself up and tried to look important as he knocked on the huge front door.

There was a long pause, but Leo knew that Mary did not move around very quickly, so he waited patiently. Eventually he heard the sound of her stick tap-tapping on the tiled hall floor.

"Well now, what have we here?" she asked, a broad smile breaking out on her wrinkled face.

"Nita's in hospital," Leo blurted out, "She fell and hurt herself."

The smile on Mary's face disappeared immediately.

"Oh, my goodness! Is she badly hurt?"

Leo shook his head. "I don't think so, but I don't really know. Mum says she doesn't think she'll be home for two or three days."

"But what happened? Look, Leo, would you like to come in and tell me all about it?"

In the warm kitchen Leo sat at the table, a drink of lemonade in front of him. He had told Mary all he knew, which wasn't a lot, and she now sat opposite him, drumming her fingers on the table.

"Oh, that poor little girl, I'll have to get John or Barbara to take me to see her."

Leo looked up.

"Can I come with you?"

"Oh, I'm sorry, dear, they don't allow children in hospitals. I'll tell you what, though, why don't you paint her a pretty picture? Something bright to cheer her up and I'll take it in to her."

Leo jumped up, thrilled with the idea.

"I'll go home and finish what I was doing this morning. It's a picture of the Lone Ranger. Nita'll like that."

Mary doubted it. "You don't think she'd like a picture of some flowers or maybe a cat or a dog better?" she suggested gently.

"Oh no, I don't think so." Leo was putting on his coat, he was eager to get home and finish his picture. "Shall I bring it back when I've done it?"

Mary looked out of the window, at the darkening sky.

"No, dear. It will be dark soon. I'll get my son, John, to call at your house and pick it up on our way to the hospital. Which house is it you live in?"

"It's the bungalow at the bottom of the hill. 'Larksong'. You can't miss it, it's painted yellow.

"Larksong? That's a pretty name. Do you get many Larks in your garden?" Mary asked.

Leo didn't know, and said so. "We get lots of birds but I only know the ones we have lots of, like sparrows and blackbirds. Mum likes them. She feeds them and talks to them."

"Well, we'll be at your house about seven o'clock, all being well. Look out for the car, won't you? It's a big, black one."

Leo knew the car, all the village children did. It was bigger and better than any other vehicle in the village and most of the boys declared themselves 'dead jealous' of it.

On his way back down the hill he met Shirley coming up the hill together with Jenny and David Jermain.

"Hello, Leo. Where have you been?" Shirley asked

"I've been to see M...The Witch," he said.

"I don't believe you." David frowned. "You wouldn't go up there on your own."

"I have so." Leo was indignant. "And what's more I had a drink in her kitchen."

"Oh, Leo, don't fib."

They didn't believe him, that was obvious.

"I did too. And if you don't believe me you can watch our house at seven o'clock, because her son's bringing her round in their car."

Shirley burst out laughing.

"Witches don't have sons, didn't you know?"

"Oh, yes they do. Just come round and you'll see." Leo started to cry, he never told lies, his Mum had taught him it was wrong, and he hated it when people thought he was lying.

"Aw, don't cry," Jenny stepped forward and put her arm round him. She was a good head taller than he was and she cuddled him to her. He didn't like it much, after all, he was a boy and he didn't want to appear sissy, so he pulled away from her.

"Sorry, Leo, we didn't mean to upset you." At least David looked as though he meant it.

"That's all right," sniffed Leo, "But I *have* been inside Hill House with the witch and she *is* coming round mine tonight."

"Okay, have it your way." Shirley was already walking off, dragging Simon by the hand. "Come on you two or the shop'll be shut."

"Where are you going?" Leo asked, his tears forgotten.

"We've got to go to the post office for Shirley's Mum," Jenny explained, "She wants some stamps. See you later."

With a wave of her hand she was off and Leo continued on his way home. He still wasn't sure that the other three believed him but he hoped they would come round his tonight so that they could see he was telling the truth.

CHAPTER TWELVE

"Oh, come on, Mother, why on earth would you want to go and visit one of the village children?"

"Because she's hurt. And because she's a nice child." Mary had made up her mind and if John didn't realise by now how stubborn she could be then he was soon going to find out.

"But how on earth did you meet her?"

Mary found herself in an awkward situation. If she told John the children had been trespassing he was likely to blow his top. He didn't have a particularly high opinion of the village children as it was. On the other hand he knew she couldn't walk into the village and couldn't therefore have met them that way. In the end she opted for half-truth, half fiction.

"They came to the house," she said, "to see the dog. He'd been barking as they walked past and they were fascinated."

John looked doubtful, but she could see that he could think of no reason why she should lie.

"Well, I still don't see why you should want to go wandering round hospitals at your time of life, but if that's what you want then just let me have my tea and I'll take you.

It was sad, Mary thought. John would do anything she asked, but she did so hate asking.

Consequently she rattled around in this great house all on her own all day. She supposed if she mentioned her loneliness to John he would organise a succession of visitors for her from the local village to the president of the Darby and Joan club, but she was damned if she would ask him. Besides, now she had the children she didn't need anyone arranging other visitors for her.

While she got herself ready to go out she pondered about her son. He was a dear boy, and very good to her in his way. He and Barbara would often take her for rides in the car on sunny days; and they had brought her the radio for her room, a room which was very comfortable she had to admit. However, he did have a rather - she could only describe it as snobbish - attitude to those less fortunate than himself and tended to look down his nose at the villagers, most of whom worked on the land. He forgot that his mother had once been a serving girl and had spent her childhood years dressed in rags.

As she tied a chiffon scarf around her neck her thoughts turned to her daughter-in-law. At least Barbara was on good terms with most of the villagers. It was she who took the weekly order into the shop for that nice Joe Hughes to deliver. Joe's visit used to be the high spot of Mary's week. Someone from the outside world with whom she could exchange a bit of gossip.

She sighed as she stood up and reached for her stick. John wouldn't be ready yet, but she'd go and sit in the hall and wait. It would probably annoy him unfortunately, he would feel he was being hurried along, but it would save time when he was ready if she didn't have too far to walk to the car.

***

-

"How did it happen, dear?"

Nita groaned. Her wrist hurt, she had a headache and she felt tired. Much as she loved her Mum and Dad she wished they would let her go to sleep.

"Leave her alone, love, she'll feel more like talking in the morning."

Without lifting her head from the pillow Nita smiled at her Dad. Thank Heavens. He understood. Her Mum leaned over and she felt soft fingers on her forehead as hair was brushed out of her eyes.

"Sorry, Nita. We'll let you sleep if you want to. We'll just sit here until they throw us out, but we'll be back tomorrow."

"Thanks, Mum." She closed her eyes and drifted thankfully to sleep.

"Why, Hello, Mrs. Soames." Dan stood up he saw the elderly woman enter the ward, leaning heavily on the cane she always used, and guided by a younger man Dan recognised as her son whose name he couldn't remember. "What on earth are you doing here?"

Mary Soames glanced at the bed. "Oh, so she's *your* daughter is she? Well, Daniel Evans, I've come to visit her."

"To visit Nita? I didn't know you knew her." Dan suddenly remembered his manners. "Oh, I'm sorry, Mrs. Soames, I don't know if you've met my wife, Maureen. Maureen, this is Mrs. Soames; she lives at Hill House and has done as long as I can remember."

Mary Soames nodded and smiled at Maureen. "And this is my son, John, who kindly brought me here."

"Please, sit down." Dan moved away from his seat to enable the old lady to sit down. He was at a loss for words; unable to understand why Mrs. Soames and her son should be here visiting Nita. The Soames' had always been a wealthy family, and although Mrs. Soames had always seemed friendly enough, she never seemed to get out these days and her son and daughter-in-law kept pretty much to themselves.

"Well, well, what have you been doing to yourself?" Dan watched as the woman leant over Nita and his daughter opened her eyes and smiled.

"I didn't know you knew Mrs. Soames, Nita?"

Nita's eyes swivelled to her father and she opened her mouth to speak but Mrs. Soames cut her short.

"Call me Mary, Daniel. No point in standing on ceremony. And my son's name's John." She waved a hand in the direction of the window where her son was gazing out into the darkness.

"Your daughter and her friend called at the house one day when our dog was barking." Mary explained, "I gather young Leo is a keen animal lover and wanted to see our hound." She smiled at Nita and somehow Dan felt that he wasn't hearing all the truth. He instinctively knew that his daughter had been up to mischief but decided to leave the questioning for later.

"Oh, Nita," Maureen leant forward, a stern expression on her face. "You know you shouldn't have troubled people like that."

"Oh, it was no trouble," Mary said, "It was nice to have visitors. I don't get many."

She sounded wistful and Dan wondered why her son suddenly turned round and stared at his mother, a puzzled expression on his face.

"We're coming to see you again," Nita said sleepily.

"I hope so. In fact, if it weren't for Leo, I wouldn't be here now. He came and told me about your accident himself. How does it feel, by the way?"

"It's sore," Nita complained.

"I expect it is. Well, here's something to make it feel a little better." Mary opened her huge handbag and pulled out a large paper bag.

"I didn't know what sort of sweets you liked, so there's all different sorts in here." She put the bag on the locker. "I hope that's all right?" she said anxiously to Maureen.

Maureen smiled. "Oh, yes. I don't think we'll worry too much what Nita eats while she's in here. It really is very kind of you, Mrs. Soames."

"Mary." The other woman corrected. "Well, we won't stay any longer, I can see the sister's got her eye on us and is probably about to come over and tell us there's only two visitors allowed at one time." She blew a kiss at Nita. "Hurry up and get well, dear."

"I will." Nita smiled and watched as Mary and her son left the ward.

"I'm sorry, I forgot to tell you..." she began.

"That's all right, love. You don't have to explain now." Dan leant over and kissed his daughter on the forehead. "You go back to sleep and maybe when we're out of here we'll invite your friend to tea."

"Oh, Dan, we couldn't!" Maureen sounded horrified but Dan couldn't see any problem.

"I don't see why not."

"Well - it just wouldn't seem right. I mean, they're hardly the same class as us, are they?"

"Class? What's class? My mum could remember Mary Soames when she used to run around Mill Lane barefoot."

"Really?" Even Nita was interested.

"That's right, when she was a little 'un she used to play with my Mum and her brothers right along the village street. She had quite a few brothers and sisters herself I believe and eventually she went into service at Hill House where she caught the eye of old Dick Soames - or young Dick Soames as I suppose he was then - who did the rare thing of marrying her before he bedded her."

"Dan!" Maureen nodded in Nita's direction, but luckily their daughter was back in the land of dreams and had not heard her father's rather risqué remark.

"Talking of which," Dan said, a glint in his eye, "Isn't it time we went home?"

"Oh, you." Maureen complained good-naturedly, but he noticed she was quick enough to kiss her daughter goodbye and take his arm.

***

"What do you want?"

Martha took a step back. She hadn't expected Harry to answer the door and his belligerence was almost palpable.

"Well?"

Martha pulled herself together. After all, she was doing nothing wrong, just visiting a friend.

"I'd like to see Belinda, please."

"You can't. She's not here."

"Oh. Well, do you know when will she be back?"

"I don't know but I shouldn't hold your breath if I were you. Look," he took a step forward and Martha fell back, afraid that he might hit her, "I know who you are. You're that stupid, interfering old woman that's been filling my wife's head with bad ideas. We don't want your kind round here, disturbing innocent people, so get back to your pit and stay there!"

He slammed the door and Martha stood on the path, trembling. How dare he speak to her like that? And what did he mean, 'filling his wife's head with bad ideas'. Surely Belinda hadn't told him of the talks they'd had. Martha turned sadly away. It looked as though her friend had betrayed her and, worse, it looked as though Belinda had been taken in completely by Harry, who, if his behaviour just now was anything to go by, had no more reformed than a lion stops roaring.

Martha walked thoughtfully towards the village shop. She had decided to call and see if Belinda was all right when the younger woman hadn't turned up for her usual Thursday morning visit. Having seen Harry, Martha was no less worried for her friend's safety. Harry could have murdered her and cut her up and buried her in the garden for all anyone would know. Martha shuddered at the turn her thoughts were taking, although she felt they were justified.

As she reached the shop she decided that, although there was nothing she really wanted at the moment, she might learn something from a chat with Hannah Hughes. Luckily the shop was empty and Hannah was happy to talk. Martha listened impatiently to the story of the little Evans girl who was now in hospital, heard how the Hughes' were planning a holiday in Southend, discovered that eleven was a very awkward age for girls judging by the stories Hannah related about her Shirley, waited while Jenny Elliot was served with a jar of marmalade and was rewarded when Hannah finally mentioned Belinda.

"She's gone to get her hair done," Hannah confided. "Apparently her husband's persuaded her to go to Tiffany's in town.

"My, isn't that very expensive?" Martha wanted to know.

"I believe it is. And he's taking her out to dinner as well."

Martha was as surprised as Hannah obviously intended her to be.

"I never thought I'd live to see the day!" she exclaimed.

"Me neither," said Hannah. "I gather it's their wedding anniversary or something.

That's right, thought Martha, she had forgotten that their anniversary was in February. Not that Harry had ever made anything of it in the past. Still, she supposed this year they had extra cause for celebration.

It was odd but for some reason Martha had expected Harry Miles to be annoyed that Belinda was pregnant. He was the sort of self-centred man who wanted all his wife's attention and couldn't bear to share it, even with his own child. Now it seemed as though she may have been wrong, it may have altered his treatment of Belinda, at least, for the better.

She thanked Hannah for the butter which she had used as her excuse for going into the shop and which was now beginning to melt in the warmth of her hands and returned to her bungalow with a lighter heart.

***

Beneath her dryer in the hairdressers Belinda was revelling in the feeling of being pampered and relaxed. The good spell that she and Harry were going through appeared to be lasting and she was beginning to lose her mistrust of him. He had seemed thrilled to pieces with the news about her pregnancy, which had surprised her, in the past he had always shied away from the subject when she had tried to suggest that they try for a baby.

In retrospect she thought it might have turned out for the better that they waited until now to bring a small new life into their home. There had been times in their marriage when she would have feared for a child's safety when Harry was having one of his 'spells' but now she felt she could at least put that worry from her mind.

The only cloud on her horizon was Harry's absolute insistence that she have nothing more to do with Martha Skingsley. He had called Martha an 'Interfering old busy-body whose only pleasure in life was meddling in other folk's business' and for a moment, when Belinda had dared to disagree with him, she had seen the dangerous gleam in Harry's eye that at one time would have caused her to duck from the fist that inevitably would follow. This time, though, she watched as he visibly made the effort and controlled his temper.

"I will not have any wife of mine having anything to do with such a nosy old cow. Is that clear?"

His voice still held a trace of menace and Belinda decided that discretion was the better part of valour.

"Yes, dear," she said meekly, and then in final protest, "But I must go and tell her - and explain...."

"No!" he roared. "You will have nothing more to do with her. All right?" He leant towards her and his bulging eyes stared into hers.

"All right," she said submissively, annoyed at her own lack of character, or bravery, or whatever it took to stand up to Harry. But if it came to a choice, which it obviously had, then she must obey her husband.

It was a shame, she thought, she had been looking forward to Martha being there throughout the pregnancy. She knew the older woman had no children, but she was kind and sympathetic and would have been a great support during the daytime while Harry was at work. Why, she had promised to knit a complete layette for the baby and Belinda had hoped to persuade her to be a Godmother when the baby was christened. Now she didn't know who she would be able to have; she had no other friends.

The tear that trickled down her cheek dried swiftly in the warm air from the dryer.

***

"There's a meeting in the Church Hall tonight," Des said as he sipped at the coffee Daphne had just made, "June wanted to know if you'd go with her."

Daphne looked up; she was surprised that June would want to involve herself with the goings-on in the village.

"Yes, of course I will. What's it about?"

"It's about the car park. You know, the Church car park or the Church Car Park that was, to be more accurate."

"Oh, Des, I don't know that I want to get involved in all that."

Des leaned back in his chair. "I can't say I blame you, really. It's just that June has said she wants to get involved with village life when she lives here and there's no time like the present to get started. I would have preferred her not to get immediately involved with something quite so controversial, but you know June, once she's got an idea about something there's no stopping her."

There was a note of pride in his voice but Daphne scarcely heard it, she was busy digesting what he had said.

"When she lives here? Des, are you trying to tell me you and she are getting married?"

She found it quite endearing that Des blushed as he admitted that was exactly what he was trying to tell her.

"I asked her last night and she accepted with almost unseemly alacrity. There doesn't seem an awful lot of point in waiting too long, after all, I've already got a home and family, so we're thinking of getting wed in June."

"Oh, Des, that's wonderful news." She put her hands out and grabbed one of his. "I'm really pleased for you, you've got yourself a lovely girl there."

He nodded. "Yes, I know. Don't think for a moment I'm not aware how lucky I am. I've already been blessed with one wonderful wife, and now it looks as though I've found myself another special person." He gave himself a visible shake and Daphne was reminded of how thoughts of his previous wife always upset him. At least now he'd found someone who, although they'd never replace his dead love in his life, would at least fill a void.

"Anyway," Des continued, " how about this meeting tonight? I know it may not be your cup of tea but June would really like to go and get her teeth into something. You don't have to say anything if you don't want to, it's just so she's got someone to introduce her around. You know what it's like going somewhere when you don't know anyone else."

Daphne nodded. "I do indeed. I don't know, Des, it's not that I mind putting in my ten penn'orth in the discussion, rather that I'm afraid I'll be on the wrong side."

"Oh?"

"Yes. You see, I think Ken Barrett is perfectly in the right to fence off his ground."

"Oh, I see. Well, put like that perhaps you're right. I'm not a Church go-er as you know, Daph, but this chap seems to have upset all those who travel to Church in a car and a few of those who don't too, just for the heck of it. Still, if that's the way you feel, I'll tell June you'd rather not go."

He got up and Daphne put out a restraining arm.

"No, don't do that Des. Thinking about it I think it may be a good idea if I do go. Mr. Barrett might need someone to speak on his behalf. I don't suppose anyone's told him about the meeting?"

Des shook his head and smiled ruefully, "That doesn't seem likely."

"Well, tell June I'll be there. I'll have to see Martha about sitting with Leo but that shouldn't be a problem."

"No need. Bring Leo round and he can stay at ours for the night."

"Thanks, Des, I was hoping you'd say that, he does enjoy spending the night at your house. See you later then."

Daphne waited until Des was out of the garden gate and she closed the door and leant against it. She'd have to plan what she was going to say at tonight's meeting, she had an uncanny feeling that she might be the only one supporting Ken Barrett's rights.

And he wouldn't even know.

CHAPTER THIRTEEN

"I know this meeting's going to be held in the Church hall, but I bet There's a few un-Christian words bandied about there tonight."

Joe looked across at his wife from his position behind the counter.

"Are you going then?" He hoped she wasn't. Hannah looked tired. Partly, he knew, because of the hours she had to work and also because of the added burden that Shirley was causing at the moment. If Hannah decided to go to the meeting tonight it would mean that she would have to rush out as soon as the shop was closed. He thought she ought to stay in and try and get her feet up and he said so.

"I'm all right," she protested. "Besides, it will do me good to get out of the house and talk to some different people."

Joe stopped himself from pointing out that she talked to different people all day. He thought he knew what she meant, anyway. She needed to get away from the house and shop. Maybe she was right; a change of scenery *would* do her good. At least he got to go out when he took the deliveries, and he had the chance to sit and chat to some of his customers leisurely, knowing that the shop would run perfectly well without him.

Joe was an old-fashioned man in that he would really prefer that his wife stayed at home while he went out and worked to support the family, but things just hadn't worked out that way. He wanted his own business, having tried working for other people and hating it. At least with the shop he felt he only had himself to answer to. However, he couldn't afford to pay outside staff, which meant that he had to rely on Hannah to assist him, and he had to admit he'd been more than lucky in his choice of wife. She had taken to shop work like a duck to water, and had given far more than he expected of her. In fact now, although he wouldn't dream of admitting it to Hannah or anybody else, he felt that it was she who ran the shop while *he* assisted *her*. He thought it was probably quite fortunate that Hannah had no head for paper-work and so all that side of things was left up to him. It meant that at least he felt that he still had ultimate control.

Added to the hard work that Hannah put in for the shop, she also managed to bring up their two children admirably, plus run the house and cook the meals and do the washing and mending.

Joe sighed with satisfaction and felt himself plump up like a well-fed bird.

His thoughts were interrupted by his daughter, who flounced out through the door that led to their living quarters.

"I'm going out," she announced as she walked through the gap between the counters, her head in the air.

Hannah looked round from where she was re-stocking the sweet counter.

"Have you finished your jobs?" she asked.

"Yes."   Shirley's mono-syllabic reply still managed to convey a great deal of sullenness and Joe decided it was time to step in.

"What's the problem?" he asked, addressing both of them.

"No problem."   Shirley hung her head and appeared to be speaking to the floor.

"Look at me when I'm speaking to you."   Joe raised his voice and his daughter raised her head correspondingly.

"It's all right, Joe.   Let her go."   Hannah sounded resigned and Shirley didn't wait for further permission from her father, she stalked out of the shop and when Hannah called after her "Be back by five for your tea." there was no reply.

"There's still trouble then?" Joe asked.

Hannah sighed.   "It's just her whole attitude," she complained, "She barely does what she's told, and what she does do she does with such a bad grace. It's not as though I ask her to do much, just make her bed and a little washing up, but I just don't seem to be making any headway."

Joe would have gone round to his wife and given her the cuddle he thought she obviously needed, but Daphne Taylor and her son came in then, swiftly followed by other customers, and the moment passed.

***

"Why don't you go out and play?" Fred Little asked his daughter.

"Oh, how can I, Dad? I don't know anyone."

"No, and you won't get to know anyone unless you make an effort. Come on, love, why don't you go for a walk round the village. You never know who you might bump into."

"No thanks, Dad, I'd rather stay here."

It was going to be an uphill struggle, Fred knew. His daughter hadn't wanted to move here in the first place; had kicked against the thought of leaving all her friends and changing schools. Still, she'd sat the eleven plus before they moved, so she wouldn't be losing any important ground, and he thought it was important that she changed to the local school before the term ended. That way she'd already have some friends when she moved to senior school in September.

"Well, would you like me to invite someone to tea?" Fred asked, "I know that the lady in the village shop has a daughter about your age."

Caroline looked up from the book she was reading, exasperation showing on her face.

"I really am perfectly happy here, Dad. I'll have plenty of time to make friends when I start that crummy school."

Fred knew he should have reprimanded his daughter for that remark, but he had to agree with her that the school didn't look very impressive. It appeared to consist of several prefabricated buildings that looked likely to blow away in a high wind. He had asked around the village, though, and had discovered the educational reputation of the school was quite high, and work on a permanent building was expected to start later in the year.

He decided to leave Caroline to her own devices and went to find Josephine who was, as he had guessed she would be, rearranging the things in the kitchen cupboards. They'd only been in the house three days and Josephine had emptied and repacked the cupboards at least half-a-dozen times, explaining that she had to have everything in 'sensible places', by which he assumed she meant in appropriate places for where she'd need to use them.

She looked up when he came in. "Hello, dear," she said, "Would you like a cup...?" Without waiting for an answer she stood up and looked round for the kettle. He didn't know why she always imagined he wanted a cup of tea if he went into the kitchen. Still, never mind, a nice cuppa would clear the dust from his throat. He settled at the table.

"I've been up in the loft."

"Have you, dear?"

"There's a heap of rubbish up there. Lucky we live near the dump, I should imagine that's where most of it will end up. Still, I'll take it all down in the yard where you'll be able to have a look at it, then if there's anything you fancy keeping you can."

Josephine smiled at him. "No valuable works of art up there, are there?" She had found the kettle, which had obviously boiled recently as she was already pouring boiling water into the teapot.

"I shouldn't think so," he said, "Although you never know. Still, I had a bit of a quick look round when the builders were here, and I never saw anything that looked as if it might be worth anything. It's mainly old furniture and kids toys. I can never understand why people leave things like that. After all, if they were important enough to store all those years, then surely they were important enough to take with them or sell when they left."

"I wonder what happened...." Josephine carefully carried the two cups and saucers to the table, setting one carefully down in front of Fred.

"To the people who used to live here?" Fred finished for her. He was used to her leaving sentences unspoken and generally knew what she was saying. "I asked around and apparently they emigrated. Decided not to sell the house in case they wanted to come back. Now I think they've decided they're pretty much settled in Australia, so they thought it was time they sold." He picked up his cup. "Lucky for us they did."

He smiled at Josephine. "Your hair looks pretty today." he said and was rewarded by a beam of happiness. She loved being given compliments and he found it easy to do. He thought his wife was the most beautiful creature in the world. And her hair did look pretty today, all soft and bouncy.

He put his cup down and gazed out of the window. There was a lot of work to be down in the garden but he knew Josephine would enjoy pottering around out there once she had got the kitchen organised. He was well satisfied with the way things were progressing. He wasn't too worried about Caroline. She was shy, that was her biggest trouble, but once she was put in a situation where she couldn't avoid other people, such as starting a new school, she actually made friends very easily.

"Well," he eased himself up out of the chair; his body was still aching from moving all the furniture and he was being careful how he moved, "I'd better go and get on."

"Isn't they're something...." Josephine looked up at him.

"No, I don't think there's anything else I ought to be doing at the moment. Give me a call when you're ready and I'll come down and give you a hand to get dinner." He dropped a kiss on his wife's upturned face and headed back to the loft.

***

The talk had been going on seemingly interminably although the meeting had only been open about an hour, and tempers were frayed. Daphne was tired. She pushed back her hair, which was falling across her face and leaned back in her chair. June, on her right, was saying her piece now; Daphne was satisfied that, thanks to the little chat she and June had before the meeting, June's words were neither as harsh nor as adamant as they might have been.

"Surely," June was saying, "There's some sort of law about custom and practice which this situation would come under? Couldn't someone find out about it?"

218

"That's all very well," grumbled Sam Elliot, "But why should we be put to all this trouble by some interfering outsider. Begging your pardon, ma'am. I didn't mean no offence."

June smiled. "None taken."

Daphne had introduced June at the beginning of the meeting, explaining that she was to marry Des Palmer who, although not a regular Church-goer, had lived all his life in the village and was well known. Obviously Sam, once he had spoken, had realised that June herself was an outsider who was interesting herself - interfering, it could be called - in the life of the village.

"Has anyone actually approached Mr. Barrett and put forward our point of view?" Maureen Evans asked. She was there with Dan and their neighbour, Sally Jermain.

Everyone looked at everybody else in surprise; it appeared that it hadn't occurred to them to actually approach Ken Barrett themselves.

"I'll have a word with him if you like," Daphne found herself saying.

There was a murmur of voices.

"That don't seem right," Sam Elliot mumbled.

"Can't send a woman to do a man's job," Jim Grigson agreed.

"Good for you, Daphne," June said.

"I think that's a good idea." Maureen beamed across the table, "What do you think, dear?" She turned to her husband who had remained fairly quiet throughout the proceedings.

He nodded. "I think Daphne might fit the bill admirably," he said in his quiet voice, and Daphne smiled gratefully at him. "I think she will be tactful but sympathetic," Dan continued, "And I'm sure she'll be in no danger at all. After all, I don't think any of us suspect Mr. Barrett of being a homicidal maniac do we?" He looked round the table where people shook their heads.

"Well, I think it ought to be dealt with by a man," Sam Elliot grumbled.

"So are you volunteering then, Sam?" Hannah smiled sweetly at him and didn't seem surprised when he shook his head.

"I don't want to go tangling with the likes of him," he muttered, "You women get on with it if you want to."

"Okay, we will." Hannah agreed. She seemed to have been nominated the unofficial chairman of the meeting, probably due to the fact that everyone knew her and the fact that there were far more women than men present at the meeting. Daphne had questioned this, and had learnt that there was an important football match on that evening, and most of the men had volunteered to baby sit in order to listen to the radio.

"However," Hannah continued, "Before we send one of our number into the 'Lion's Den' as it were, why don't we write him a letter?"

"Waste of time," someone said. Hannah knew, without looking in his direction, that the grumble came from Sam, and she heard the wallop as Jenny slapped his arm, the sound of flesh on leather was unmistakable, as was the hushed whisper "Shut your moaning, Sam."

"Well?" Hannah looked round the table, at the nodding heads. Everyone seemed in agreement.

"I wonder if we could ask you to write the letter, Daphne?" Hannah knew that her own writing was almost illegible and that it never made sense even when it was deciphered.

"All right then. I'll write the letter and bring it into the shop so you and Joe can check it's okay before I send it."

"Right." Hannah looked round the table. "Shall we meet here again next Saturday to catch up with developments?"

There was a murmur of approval   "Well," Hannah got up, "If that's decided, I'd better get home and see what my lot's been up to.

Daphne walked home with June. They were joined by Sam and Jenny Elliot. "Bloomin' waste of time that was," Sam said.

"Oh, I don't know, at least we're doing something constructive." June said.

"Don't mind him, June, he's only happy when he's miserable." Jenny linked arms with her husband and patted him playfully on the chin, "Aren't you, darling?"

His muttered reply was lost in the chill of the late February night and Daphne tucked her gloveless hands in her pockets in an effort to keep the blood circulating.

"I just hope the letter does some good," she said.

"What, and deny the rest of the village the chance to complain? It'd take away their excuse for a good old get together and gossip."

Daphne had to agree, if only to herself, that maybe Sam did have something there. The meeting tonight had been more than just a discussion about car parking; it had been a chance for everyone to have a good old natter with a cup of tea or coffee to wet the whistle.

"Still," she said aloud, "It would be nice if we get the parking spaces back without too much bad feeling.

"I'm sure we will," said June, "I daresay Ken Barrett doesn't even realise the trouble he's caused. Probably had a copy of his deeds and marked off the boundary, not knowing about the parking."

Daphne doubted it; she thought Ken Barrett was probably well aware of everything that went on in the village. He didn't seem the type of man to go around blindly. Still, she decided to write the letter as soon as she got home and get it over with. Then she'd be able to call at Joe and Hannah's on the way to Church in the morning and, if they approved, she could drop it in the door of the Big House on her way to Church.

Sam and Jenny left them at the top of Clay Lane and Daphne and June continued alone.

"Funny couple," June said, "He's as miserable as a wet weekend and yet she'd a really lively soul."

"Daphne nodded. "That's true," she said, "and yet he worships the ground she walks on. Watch him next time they're together, he never takes his eyes off her."

"Ah, that's nice."

"Well, you're okay, you've got Des. He seems pretty keen on you."

June smiled, "He does, doesn't he? Which reminds me, I've been meaning to as you.... I know you and Des were pretty friendly before I came on the scene. I haven't trod on anyone's toes, have I?"

"Good Lord, no. Honestly, June, there was never anything between Des and I except friendship. Even that probably wouldn't have come about were it not for Leo and Benny, but that's all there ever was."

"Good, I'm glad. I wouldn't like to feel you resented me for any reason, I'd like us to be friends as well."

"I thought we were!"

June grinned. "That's all right then."

They stopped outside Des' cottage.

"Coming in for a drink?" June asked.

Daphne shook her head. "I don't think so, if you don't mind, June. Think I'll get home and get this letter written."

"Good idea. See you in Church then."

Daphne waited until June opened the front door before turning and waving goodbye, then she continued home. She was already composing the letter in her mind.

***

Dan and Maureen walked home arm in arm after the meeting, chatting to Sally as they walked. They were anxious to get home to Nita, who was out of hospital now and seemed in good spirits. Nonetheless, neither of them had really wanted to go out and leave her for long. Scarlett and Eric had agreed to stay in and 'baby-sit', a phrase which really annoyed Scarlett's young sister, and both Dan and his wife were pleased that the meeting had not gone on too long. It was still only nine thirty, and although Nita should have been tucked up in bed half an hour ago they both suspected she wouldn't be.

"Daphne Taylor's come out of her shell recently, hasn't she?" Sally commented.

"She certainly has," Maureen agreed. "I don't know what's caused it, although I rather thought she and Des Palmer had something going at one time, then this June appears and it turns out he's going to marry her. Still, he certainly seems to have helped Daphne somehow, until they got friendly Daphne would hardly say boo to a goose."

"Hasn't she got a son?" Sally wanted to know.

"Yes, Leo. Our Nita's quite friendly with him, he's a nice enough boy, although there's something wrong with him - his mind, you know," she tapped her head to demonstrate, "Still, Daphne dotes on him and they're very close; she looks after him very well, and he doesn't really seem aware that he's different to the other children, although, of course, he goes to that special school in town."

"Well, I think she's bitten off more than she can chew this time," said Sally, "That Ken Barrett seems a nasty piece of work."

"Now, I won't hear a word said against him," Dan put in. "He took our Nita to the hospital and could have saved her life."

"That's right, he did, didn't he?" Sally remembered.

"And it was Daphne who persuaded him," pointed out Maureen. "Perhaps she has a way with her."

"Mmm," Dan pretended to consider, "I suppose she is rather attractive." He grinned at his wife and shied away from the playful punch she threw. "But not as attractive as you, my lovely wife." He hugged her to him, and they continued their walk in the crisp night air.

CHAPTER FOURTEEN

"Hannah, you look exhausted!"

Joe stood up abruptly when Hannah entered the room, shocked at how tired she looked. "Why on earth did you go to that stupid meeting?"

"Because, Joe Hughes, I live in this village and want to be part of what goes on here." Her words were firm but she sounded breathless and Joe hurried over to her side.

"Here, love, come and sit down and put your feet up. I'll make you a nice cup of tea."

"Something stronger wouldn't go amiss."

Joe stopped in mid-stride on his way out to the kitchen. Hannah must be feeling odd if she was suggesting alcohol. A small glass of sherry at Christmas and anniversaries was usually her limit.

"All right, love. I'll put the kettle on and then I'll find you a drop of brandy."

By the time he came back in the room Hannah was asleep. The unusual pallor of her face and her absolute stillness nearly made his heart stop for a moment, but then he noticed the gentle rise and fall of her breathing and he relaxed again. He pulled the coffee table over next to her chair and put the brandy on it. The tea could wait until she woke naturally; he didn't want to disturb her. He sat back down in his own chair and resumed reading the paper, glancing up at Hannah every now and again. When he realised he had read the same paragraph three times and still hadn't taken any of it in he folded the paper and laid it carefully on the coffee table. Leaning back, he watched Hannah sleeping and wished life could always be as peaceful for her.

For some reason he was reminded of their honeymoon, remembered how young and carefree she'd been - they'd both been. The didn't have much money and had spent a reasonably priced week at the seaside. It was wonderful. Joe thought it came close to being the best week of his life. They went on every ride on the pier, played the penny machines in the amusement arcade, listened to the band in the pavilion in the afternoons and, in the evening, after an enormous meal served by their landlady, had retired to their room where they had explored and discovered each other's bodies and learnt new ways of expressing their love for each other. Hannah was shy at first, Joe recalled, but she swiftly responded to the desires of her body. Not that he had been experienced, a few gropes in the back of the cinema with previous girlfriends had been his limit, but Hannah hadn't even allowed that much while they were courting. And when they got married he was glad she hadn't; it meant they came to each other fresh, and every move had been electric with excitement. Together they reached the peak of fulfilment and their lives had continued with the same heady excitement for months afterwards.

Seven and a half months, to be exact. Shirley had been conceived on their honeymoon and arrived early - a tiny, wrinkled package of pink flesh. He couldn't remember exactly how much she weighed, men didn't remember that kind of detail, but he knew she was so tiny, so fragile and delicate that she won his heart immediately, even before they were able to hold her.

Joe remembered the days of worry when they weren't sure Shirley would survive, and the day she first wrapped her little fingers round his thumb and he felt her strength and knew she'd be okay.

It was soon after Hannah brought the baby home that Joe's Dad died. They had all known he had a heart problem that could take him any time; it was something they had learnt to live with. In the end, it was almost as though he'd waited to see his grand-daughter before he gave up and surrendered to his traitorous body.

When everything was sorted Joe found he had been left a small inheritance. Not a fortune, but enough for a down-payment on a little business. When the village shop came up for sale around the same time it seemed like fate.

Much as Joe was satisfied with the move it meant a lot of hard work and this, coupled with bringing up the children, played havoc with their love-life and sometimes he regretted the passing of those early days. Then he reminded himself that in the place of that first, heady excitement, was now something much sweeter: a joining, a coupling of spirits; a feeling of belonging, of being part of another; a sharing of joy as well as trouble; a partner, a support, and a precious love.

"Penny?"

Hannah's voice brought him back to the present.

"Sorry, love, I was just thinking."

"Well, how about thinking of that cup of tea?" Hannah reached down for the brandy and held it out to him. "I don't think I fancy this now, you can have it if you like."

"Are you sure? It would probably do you good, you know."

Hannah stood up. "I'm sure. I think the tea will do me a lot more good. Mind you, I think I'm ready for bed. Fancy bringing the tea upstairs?"

Joe nodded agreement and Hannah walked slowly out of the room. As Joe heard her walk heavily up the stairs he decided that, if she felt no livelier in the morning, he'd get her to go and see Doctor Jean;

maybe a tonic would be all she needed. He downed the brandy in one gulp and winced as its warmth hit his stomach, then went through to the kitchen to make the tea.

***

Dear Mr. Barrett, Daphne read,

I have been asked to write to you on behalf of members of the village who use their cars for visiting our Church. You may not be aware that it has been customary for these visitors to use the concrete area at the back of your property for parking. We appreciate that this ground does, in fact, belong to you, but we would be very grateful if you could allow the custom to continue. Removal of the fencing recently erected would allow access to this parking area.

We would be very grateful for your co-operation in this matter and assure you that no visitor will overstep the confines of the parking area or trespass further on your land.

Yours sincerely,
Daphne Taylor.

Daphne could think of no other way she could word the letter to make it sound less of a cheek, for a cheek is what she thought it was. Asking somebody to allow access to their land and writing a letter which implied a right to this access amounted to a downright liberty, in Daphne's eyes. The only reason she had agreed to write the letter was because she thought she might temper the wording a little bit more than some of the others who were at the meeting who thought the idea of Ken Barrett taking 'their' land away was preposterous, and who couldn't wait to tell him so.

Satisfied, she put the letter in an envelope and addressed it, then put it in her handbag so she wouldn't forget it in the morning.

It was strange at night being in the bungalow without Leo, but she was getting used to it, and he loved spending the night with his friend. Benny was good for her son, there was no doubting that. In the past year she had seen Leo grow in confidence. When she had discovered he had been up to Hill House and told Mrs. Soames about Nita's accident Daphne had been annoyed at first, wondering why on earth Leo would want to bother the old lady. When she heard the full story though, she was pleased her son had been thoughtful enough to let Mrs. Soames know. It was for sure that nobody else in the village would have done the same. Why should they? Only Leo, Nita and Mary Soames had known of the strange friendship that apparently existed between the three of them.

Daphne snuggled under the covers of her bed. She'd have to invite Mary Soames to tea one night. Leo would like that. With that thought her eyes closed and she fell asleep, but her dreams were not of Mary Soames or the children. Instead, Ken Barrett's searching glance haunted her night-time hours.

***

Belinda never saw it coming. Never heard the alarm bells or noticed the warning gleam in Harry's eyes. Things had been so good for so long that she had forgotten to be alert; had relaxed her guard, so that when the fist came there was no protection.

It had been a good week until then. The dinner on their anniversary had gone well, Harry had been on his best behaviour, hadn't belched or passed wind once during the time they were at the restaurant, and had even managed to use the right utensils for each course.

He had drunk only a few glasses of wine, and, after the meal was over, had rushed to help her on with her coat. They had walked home arm in arm and she believed herself to be truly happy. She had a husband who loved and cared for her, and who would never, she was sure, ever hit her again, and a precious little person was growing inside her who would make their lives complete.

Saturday they had gone shopping. Harry seemed eager to make some purchases for their child and they h caught the bus into town where he had spent lavishly on matinee jackets and dresses, booties and mittens, rattles and mobiles, ignoring Belinda's protests when she pointed out they would be sure to be given clothes for the baby. Every woman in the village would start knitting as soon as they knew.

"I don't want charity," Harry had said, his mouth tight, "What we can't buy for our own child we'll go without."

If there was a slight frenzy about his buying Belinda chose to ignore it. She didn't question where the money came from or how they would pay the bills next month, or next week. She had always had a man to depend on and they had never let her down, had they?

That night Belinda had sat looking through the day's purchases and trying to imagine her own baby, dressed in the pink dress or the blue dungarees (Harry had bought for every eventuality).

"I'm just going up to the Lion for a few pints," Harry said, dragging his fisherman's knit pullover over his head as he walked into the room.

"Oh, Harry..." Belinda started to protest.

"It's all right, I won't be long. Want to see if Joe Grigson's up there, he owes me a pint."

"Oh, all right."

Belinda returned to her inspection of their purchases and her dreams for the future.

Harry wasn't back when Belinda went to bed at ten o'clock but she still didn't worry. He was probably having a good old chin-wag with his friends. He'd be okay.

She soon slipped into sleep, aware that the pregnancy was already making her feel tired by the evening.

The room was dark when she was yanked from her bed.

"You stupid slag!" Harry's words were slurred and her insides lurched as if their baby knew what was about to happen and was protesting its fear.

She was thrown across the room and she hit the wall with a thud and slid down, dazed, onto the floor.

"You foul bitch," the tirade continued, "Dirty whore."

Harry kicked out, his heavy boot landing in her stomach and somehow she knew the life inside of her died at that moment. She went limp, as if she, too, had slipped away from life, and Harry picked her up like a rag doll and flung her on the bed.

Dimly, as if through a heavy curtain, she heard the abuse Harry continued to hurl at her as he proclaimed the child wasn't his and that she must have lain with some other man to conceive it. She didn't even protest when he ripped her night-gown off her body and thrust himself inside her. Though the physical pain as he tore her flesh was great, it could not compare with the mental anguish she was experiencing. After he had finished he rolled off of her and within seconds he was snoring. Carefully, both because of the pain it caused her to move, and the fact that some subconscious protective instinct didn't want her to wake him, Belinda eased her way off of the bed. She pattered down the wooden stairs, her feet slipper-less, and out of the front door, which Harry hadn't bothered to lock and Belinda didn't bother to close. She crossed the almost deserted street, not noticing the Grigson's cat that ran out of her way, unaware of Joe Hughes, who looked up from putting a milk bottle out on to the doorstep and caught sight of a wraith-like figure gliding across the end of the street. At Martha's front door she knocked once, loudly, on the knocker and then, as if the survival instinct, which had kept her going, knew its work was done, she collapsed on the doorstep.

Martha was a light sleeper and the knock on the door broke easily through the dream she was having; a dream in which she was running down the street towards her family and friends where they waited, open-armed, but they never got any nearer. Waking was a cessation of frustration for her. Her feeling of relief was quickly replaced by concern. Who would come knocking on her door at this time of night?

She took her robe from the hook on the back of the door and wrapped it round her while she slipped her feet into her slippers. Switching on all the lights, she stood in the hall. "Who is it?" she called.

There was no answer and Martha opened the door carefully.

When she saw the hunched figure she gave a cry and threw the door back.

"Belinda, what's happened?"

The eyes that looked up at her were dark and heavy with pain and grief and Martha knew that any further questioning would be futile. Belinda was in no condition to speak.

Gently, she put her arms under her friend's elbows and eased her to her feet. Belinda was little help, limp and lifeless as she was, and Martha gave thanks for the muscles she had developed when caring for her parents and having to lift her father between bed and wheelchair. The muscles complained, not having been used for a while, but eventually Belinda was laying on the settee.

Martha went through to the kitchen and put the kettle on, allowing her friend a little time to recover her wits enough to tell Martha what had been going on. Not that it took much imagination; Harry had obviously been up to his old tricks.

"Here you are, dear, a nice cup of tea." Martha grimaced at the banality of the remark but held the cup of tea up to her friend's mouth and was relieved when Belinda took a few sips before pushing the cup away.

"No more," she whispered, her voice weak.

"I'll put it down here, all right?" Martha put the mug on the floor and knelt beside Belinda. She stroked back the hair that was matted on her friend's forehead and felt the damp chill of sweat.

"Do you want to tell me what happened?" she asked quietly.

"I've lost the baby." Belinda's voice was a low monotone. "I've lost the baby," she repeated.

"Are you sure?" Martha didn't know a lot about having babies and wasn't sure what physical signs there should be.

"I felt him die." Belinda said in that same, dull voice.

"Well, I'm going to find a telephone and get Doctor Jean out to see you."

Martha stood up. She expected Belinda to protest as she usually did, but the younger woman just gazed into space, almost as if she was unaware of Martha's presence.

Quickly, Martha put on her thick coat and slipped boots on her feet for quickness. Checking she had her keys and the card she kept with the doctor's 'phone number on, she hurried out of the bungalow along to the telephone box outside the Grigson's house, thinking how lucky there was one so close. Inside the box she dialled the number and waited impatiently for Doctor Jean to answer. Eventually the receiver was picked up and a sleepy voice spoke. "Dr. Meredith speaking."

"Doctor Jean, it's Martha, Martha Skingsley."

Doctor Jean's tone of voice indicated that she was instantly alert. "Martha? What's the matter?"

"It's not me, doctor, it's young Belinda Miles. She's just appeared on my doorstep. Says she's lost the baby."

"I'll be right there. You say she's at yours?"

"Yes, doctor."

"Keep her warm. Tell her I'm on my way." The connection was cut abruptly and Martha knew that by now Doctor Jean would be running for her car, dragging on clothes as she went.

Back in the bungalow Belinda hadn't moved.

Martha resumed her kneeling position beside her friend. "Doctor's coming, Belinda, you'll be all right

239

now." She remembered the doctor's instructions to keep Belinda warm and went through to her bedroom to fetch the heavy quilt. She was returning through the hall when the doorbell rang.

"Thank you for coming Doctor. Belinda's in here."

Doctor Jean nodded acknowledgement. "Thanks Martha, now how about popping the kettle on while I have a look at our young lady?" She took the quilt from Martha's arms and strode into the living room.

Martha took the hint and stayed in the kitchen even after the kettle had boiled, guessing that the doctor was respecting Belinda's privacy by not having anyone else present. When she heard the door to the living room open she put the kettle on to re-boil.

"I think we'll all have a drink," said Doctor Jean, "And a biscuit wouldn't go amiss, if you have one." She sat in the chair and rested her hands on the Formica-topped table. "Well, what can you tell me about what's been happening?"

"Me?"

"Well, I can't get anything out of that young woman in there except that she's lost the baby - which she hasn't by the way. A lot of women don't realise just how protected the baby is in the womb. Nature designed it that way. Still, judging by the bruising on her body she has a right to be scared. How did it happen, do you know?"

Martha shrugged, unwilling to betray her friend's confidence while at the same time wanting to protect Belinda.

"Hmm, won't say anything, eh?" The doctor leant forward. "Martha Skingsley, I've known you a long while and I'm pretty damn sure you know something about this mess, for that's what it is if I'm not mistaken." She leant back and picked up her cup of tea. "All right. I can't force you to tell me but I would like to ask something of you."

Martha put a tray on the table and put two cups of tea on it. "Doctor, I'll do anything I can to help Belinda. What do you want me to do?"

"Simple. Stop her going back home."

Simple! That was a laugh, thought Martha. Still, it was what she intended to do anyway, and she nodded as she placed a plate of biscuits on the tray. "I'll do my best," she promised, "If I don't succeed it won't be for want of trying."

"I'm sure that's true" The doctor picked up her tea. "Now let's see what we can do to bring young Mrs. Miles back to reality. She hasn't lost the baby, but if she intends to keep it she'd better start taking care of herself."

CHAPTER FIFTEEN

Benny came and called for Leo at ten o'clock on the Sunday morning. As usual Leo had been up for several hours during which he had scattered most of his toys round the bungalow. He was anxious to go and play with his friend but when Benny called round Leo still took the time to tidy up - to his satisfaction, anyway, before setting off down the street with Benny.

Daphne was tired, she had found sleep difficult to catch hold of the previous night, had lain awake for hours with thoughts churning in her brain. For some inexplicable reason she had found her thoughts kept returning to Derek and the brief marriage they had known. In the ensuing years since their split she had been content to live alone, bringing up Leo and sharing her life with him. Now they had both branched out; Leo - by virtue of his friendship with the head of the village "gang" - had been accepted by the local children. He was encouraged to join in their games in which the group of eight to fourteen year olds could be found sneaking round corners or tramping across fields on God knew what latest adventure. Now Daphne herself was at last breaking free of the fears and insecurities that had surrounded her. Her friendship with Des had been welcome and was even better now that it included June, but she was becoming aware of a kind

243

of loneliness. She supposed it had something to do with Des and June being a couple; however welcoming they were she was on the outside and could not share in that special something that sparked between them.

Daphne washed up the breakfast things after Leo and Benny left, looking round the good-sized kitchen as she did so. She wished she didn't owe this lovely bungalow to Derek, wished that somehow she had been self-supporting and had not had to rely on anybody else, least of all someone who had let her down so badly. Still, Derek had never faltered in his contribution to his son's well-being, she had to say that for the man. The payments were made regularly each month into her bank account.

It seemed odd to think that she didn't even know where her ex-husband lived, but that was the way they had both wanted it. She hadn't wanted to be reminded of the humiliation of his rejection. And Derek - well, he just hadn't wanted to be reminded of her.

In retrospect she wondered if he had ever felt guilty or less of a man because of Leo and his problems. In the distance brought by the passing of the years Daphne felt she could perhaps be charitable and pretend that Derek hadn't really been a low-down cheating cad but had, maybe, had his own cross to bear and had dealt with it the only way he knew how.

The day was bright with a watery, winter sun but the chill crept into the bungalow through the ill-fitting doors and windows and Daphne guessed it would be extremely cold outside. She dressed in her heavy winter coat, it was good quality and had worn well. She always bought expensive clothes on the basis they lasted longer and her wardrobe, though sparse, had survived many changing fashion seasons.

She pulled on her gloves and collected the letter to Ken Barrett from the hall table. If she left early she could call in at Hannah's on the way to Church so that she and Joe could read the letter before Daphne delivered it.

Outside the winter chill crept round her neck and she turned up her coat collar and hunched her shoulders in an effort to beat it. She walked briskly to ward off the chill and, by the time she arrived at Hannah and Joe's she could feel her cheeks glowing and her earlier tiredness disappearing in the wake of the exhilaration.

By contrast, Joe, when he answered her knock, was pale and looked as if he hadn't slept for a week. Not that Daphne noticed at first, she was busy fumbling in her handbag for the letter but when she held it out to him and lifted her gaze to his she could tell something was wrong.

245

"I've brought the letter," she said. Then, when no light of understanding registered on Joe's face, she continued, "The letter I was asked to write to Ken Barrett...about the car parking." Her hand remained held out with the letter in it like some unwanted gift.

"Joe...are you all right?"

"Oh, I'm sorry, Mrs. Taylor. It's Hannah, you see. She's not well."

"Oh, I am sorry." Daphne withdrew her hand and discreetly slipped the letter into the roomy pocket of her coat; Joe wouldn't want to be bothered with that now. "What's wrong with her? She seemed okay last night."

"What? Oh, yes, that damn meeting. Begging your pardon, Mrs. Taylor. But my Hannah shouldn't be bothering herself with things like that, not when she's so tired. It's exhaustion, you see, or so the Doctor says. I don't know what I'm going to do."

Joe seemed to be talking to himself, almost unaware of her presence and Daphne put her hand on his arm,

"Is there anything I can do, Joe?"

His gaze focused on her, "What? Oh, no... no, I don't think so, thank you ever-so kindly. I've sent young Shirley up to Maureen's, she'll help out as like as not. But it's Hannah, you see. I'm worried about Hannah."

"She'll be all right, I'm sure. Plenty of rest, did the doctor say?"

Joe nodded. "I'd best get back to her, if you don't mind."

"Of course. Give her my best wishes, won't you? Tell her I'll call and see her when she's feeling up to it."

Joe shook his head violently. "No visitors. Doctor says no visitors, not yet awhile, anyhow."

His voice was almost hysterical and Daphne's tones were, by contrast, quiet and calming as she replied. "No, I understand, Joe. I'll leave it until she's feeling better."

Joe turned back into the house, and Daphne stood on the pavement for a few minutes, thinking. Firstly she thought about Hannah and what she could do to help her and Joe. Help in the shop, that was one thing, at least while Leo was at school. Do any shopping or household chores that needed doing, that was something else. Have young Shirley and Simon round at her home to give Joe a break. Oh, yes, there was plenty she could do - and she wouldn't be the only one, either. She may not have joined in much in the local activity the last eight years, but that didn't mean she hadn't seen what was going on. She was well aware that everyone mucked in to help each other in times of crisis, and, if she would only admit it to herself, she had been the slightest bit jealous of the close-knit community. Now she was part of it, she could almost skip with happiness, but then she remembered Hannah and she sobered. She'd call in tomorrow when Joe had got used to the idea of his Hannah being ill, and they could sort something out then.

Her second problem was more immediate. What did she do about the letter? Should she deliver it to Ken Barrett without anyone else seeing it, or should she get someone else to okay it first? She was reluctant to take on herself the sole responsibility for the letter and was relieved when she saw Dan and Maureen Evans walking swiftly up the slight incline in the road, little Shirley Hughes between them. Daphne hurried towards them, smiling a greeting. "Lovely morning," she said.

"Isn't it?" Maureen smiled a response. "Not so good for Hannah, though, I'm afraid."

"So I hear. I just called to see her and Joe says he's had to have the doctor out."

"That's right, Doctor Jean was there early, I gather."

"Mum's not well."

Daphne looked down at the child, at the pinched face and the red hands. Obviously Joe had sent her out with no gloves. Men!

She crouched down so that she was on a level with Shirley. "How about one day this week you and Simon come to tea with Leo? Would you like that."

Shirley looked up at Maureen, as if seeking permission.

"That would be nice, wouldn't it, Shirley?"

"I thought it might help," Daphne stood up, "And perhaps you'd tell Joe I'd be happy to help out in the shop or do any chores; you know, anything that will be of help."

"That's kind of you, I think they'll be glad of all the help they can get. Now, if you'd excuse me, I think I'll go and see what hours Joe will be wanting me to work. See you in Church." Maureen took Shirley's hand and strode off towards the shop.

"So, Mrs. Taylor, did you decide what you're going to put in the letter?" Dan continued walking in the direction of the Church and Daphne fell into step beside him.

"Indeed I did. In fact, I have it here." Daphne pulled the envelope out of her pocket. "That's why I called at Hannah's, she was going to read it before I delivered it. I wonder, would you mind just checking it for me? Just to make sure it says what everyone wants it to say?"

"Surely." Dan took the letter and read it through. "Seems fine to me," he said, handing it back. "Dropping it in now, are you?"

"I may as well." She turned and, Dan beside her, made her way up the lane. At the entrance to the Big House she stopped.

"Here, I'll do that for you." Dan took the letter from her hand, "You carry on up to the Church. It won't be hot in there but it'll be a bit warmer than out here."

Daphne carried on gratefully. Somehow she hadn't looked forward to that walk to the door of the Big House; she had been afraid that Ken Barrett might look out and see her and know she was on the side of the enemy.

Dan caught her up as she entered the Church.

"There, that's done. I suppose we sit and wait for developments now."

"That's all we can do." Daphne helped herself to a hymn book from the pile that the Churchwarden was sorting. "Dan, will Hannah be all right?"

"Oh, yes, she'll be okay. Doctor Jean called at ours after seeing Hannah. She knows Maureen you see, and thought that Maureen would want to know what was happening. Hannah's to have complete rest for a week at least. Seems that Joe's booked a holiday for them but not for a couple of months. Poor old

Hannah just couldn't wait that long and her body rebelled. But she'll be all right after a rest, you'll see."

"That's good." Daphne went and sat in the body of the Church, a little nearer the front this time; she was finally coming out of the shadows.

Maureen just made the Church in time for the service. She had spent a difficult twenty minutes with Joe. He seemed lost without Hannah by his side and was worried beyond all reason as to how he was going to cope while she was ill. Maureen had reassured him that there would be plenty of help and she was beginning to wonder if she should be prepared for having no Joe in the shop as well as no Hannah; if he continued to behave as he was this morning he'd be no good at all.

She spotted Daphne sitting on her own in the centre of the Church and went and joined her.

"Everything all right?" whispered Daphne.

"Not really, but it'll sort itself out. Perhaps we could have a little chat after the service - if you're still prepared to help out, that is?"

"Of course."

They turned their attention to the minister although Maureen found her thoughts wandering in the sermon. Surely the Reverend Watson had preached this same thing only last year? Or something very similar, anyway.

It was unfortunate that Nita was at home at the moment. Although her hand was healing well Maureen and Dan had decided it would be wise to keep their daughter away from school for a few more days. It would only take a slight knock to open up the wound afresh and they both knew their younger child could not be counted on to be careful.

It meant that Maureen would have to limit the hours she could put in at the shop to the evenings. Once Scarlett or Dan were home she could leave Nita in their care.

Daphne had offered help and Maureen thought she would probably be good in the shop. In her head she ran through the list of other wives who could be counted on to help out: Sally Mailer, Jenny Elliot, Jan Grimes, Ann Jermain. That would do for a start. She'd call round and see Sally and Jan after the service. Jenny was here, sitting with Sam the other side of the aisle, she'd catch her afterwards.

Then there was the business of Belinda Miles to worry about. Doctor Jean had mentioned being called out to her. It seemed the good Doctor hadn't got a lot of sleep the previous night. Apparently Belinda was with Martha Skingsley, there had been some sort of trouble involving Harry, from what Maureen could gather. She ought to call at Martha's after Church as well. Oh dear, they'd be lucky if they had dinner before three o'clock today; it was no use hoping Scarlett would start the dinner, she'd be too busy pouring over the Practical Householder magazines that she and Eric had bought, and trying to decide on colour schemes.

Really Maureen supposed Miller's End was coming along very nicely. The young couple were spending all their spare time there. If the place wasn't so cold and draughty Maureen might have worried about what they were getting up to, but she was sure Scarlett was a sensible girl and wouldn't get up to mischief. Besides, she was a girl who liked comfort and Maureen couldn't imagine her giving in to gay abandon on bare floorboards. No, she was pretty sure Scarlett would save herself for her wedding night, it was something Maureen had taken care to drum into her elder daughter. She sighed, she supposed it was something she would soon have to start drumming into Nita, but she thought she may be wasting her breath, she was sure Nita would go her own sweet way. Still, at least Maureen would do her best by both her daughters.

The sound of scraping chairs as the congregation stood to their feet brought Maureen back to the present and she spent the rest of the service in devout worship.

Afterwards Daphne was stopped by several people who had been at last night's meeting and wanted to know if she'd written the letter yet. While she stopped to talk to various of them Maureen managed to intercept Jenny and Sam Elliot as the congregation filed out of the building. "Jenny, I wonder if I could have a word?"

"Aren't you coming in to the hall for coffee?" Jenny wanted to know.

"Well no. I'll have to give it a miss this morning. Hannah's not well, you see, and I'm trying to round up some help for Joe. He's gone to pieces, poor man."

Jenny looked concerned.

"Serious?" Sam asked.

"No, thank goodness. But you wouldn't think it to see poor Joe."

"Ah well, as long as there's nothing too badly wrong with the lass." Sam turned to Jenny. "You women sort things out and I'll see you at home. All right, love." He kissed his wife on the forehead and joined several other men as they made their way down the lane for their usual lunchtime pint in the Red Lion.

"Now," Jenny turned to Maureen. "What exactly would you like me to do?"

Together they sorted out the hours Jenny would work. "I'm sure the others will fit in round that,"

Maureen said, "Oh, and there's some trouble with Belinda Miles as well, I'm going round to see her shortly."

""Oh?" Jenny's simple "Oh?" was laden with curiosity and Maureen filled her in with what she knew - which didn't amount to much.

"Oh well," said Jenny as she took her leave of Maureen, "We all knew there was going to be trouble there sooner or later. Let me know if there's anything else I can do."

"I will. Thanks." Maureen turned to meet Daphne and the two women walked slowly down the lane together. When they parted, Daphne to collect Leo from Des and Maureen to continue her good works, they had decided some of the jobs Daphne would be involved in during the coming weeks. Maureen got the distinct impression that Daphne was very pleased to become an active member of the community that she had lived on the outside of for so many years.

"I'm still not sure what's going on with Belinda." Maureen flopped on to the settee. The dinner had been cooked and eaten, the washing up done and the rest of the day was hers. Nita left her chair the other side of the fireplace and came and cuddled up next to her mother and Maureen felt a sudden burst of affection for her daughter. Both her children were growing up so quickly, she knew she must make the most of the childhood still left in Nita. She put her arm round Nita and pulled her closer.

Dan looked up from his chair where he had been gazing into the fire, apparently daydreaming. "That's right, I forgot, you went to see her this morning as well, didn't you?"

Maureen had already brought Dan up to date on the Hannah and Joe situation and had been relieved that he hadn't complained about her putting in extra hours. Not that Dan complained often, but she knew that deep down he would prefer it if she didn't work to supplement the money he earned; somehow it seemed to threaten his masculinity, she couldn't work out why.

"Well, I called on Martha Skingsley, yes, but she wouldn't let me see Belinda - said the girl was too upset to see anyone just now, but if I'd like to call back in the week I'd maybe be able to see her then. Damn cheek of the woman, anyone would think she was Belinda's mother."

"Now, now. You know full well that Martha Skingsley's worth her weight in gold. You're just peeved because you couldn't find out what's happened."

Maureen felt herself blush and knew that what Dan said was true. She had wanted to know what had happened, but it wasn't just nosiness, she was genuinely concerned. Surely Dan knew that? As if he could read her mind he continued. "I know you want to help, love, but give Martha her due - the woman's an Angel in disguise. If she can't help Belinda over what ails her then nobody can."

"You're right, of course. Sorry, Dan"

"Heck, woman, don't apologise to me."

"I still think her husband's at the bottom of it. I reckon he's hit her once too often."

"Come on now, love, you don't know that for sure." He frowned and nodded towards Nita who was curled up, her feet on the settee with her head in her mother's lap. Maureen realised Dan disapproved of her talking like that in front of their daughter, even if Nita did appear to be asleep. Nonetheless, Maureen was sure she was right, Harry Miles had been beating his wife up, and it looked as though this time he may have gone too far.

"Have you considered that it may be something quite simple?" Dan asked. "The girl might be pregnant."

"Oh." Maureen hadn't considered that and she cast her mind back to the last time she had seen Belinda. Now she came to think about it, there had been a bloom about her. She had been happy, as well, happier than Maureen had seen her. "I suppose that's possible. But why would she be at Martha's, and why would she be upset?"

Dan shrugged. "Don't ask me about the working of the female mind. It's a total mystery to most males. Nonetheless, if I remember rightly, ladies can behave somewhat oddly at these times."

Maureen knew that Dan had never got over the craving she'd had for baked beans with strawberries when she was carrying Scarlett. He always maintained it was what had caused Scarlett's red hair.

"Maybe you're right. Anyway," she nudged Nita, "Who's for a game of snap?"

CHAPTER SIXTEEN

For Joe, Sunday passed in a daze. It was a day in which people came and went and made arrangements which he immediately forgot. A day in which Hannah slept, and woke, and slept again, occasionally sipping a little soup from a spoon, or some custard from the bowl which Jenny Elliot brought round at teatime, still steaming.

Joe had pulled up the stool which Hannah used to sit on when she applied her make up on the rare occasions that they were going out to somewhere special, and he spent most of Sunday sitting on it, close to Hannah. Close enough to watch the fall and rise of her breathing, to hold her hand for comfort and to be there to smile at her when she woke. Occasionally Shirley made herself known and would come into the bedroom, her younger brother tagging along behind, where Shirley would ask Joe about her mother's state of health.

Joe took time off from his vigil to open a can of soup and sat at the table with his children where he hurriedly gulped his down before taking a tray up to Hannah's room to patiently try and spoon-feed her.

He was so worried. It didn't matter that Doctor Jean had said his wife would be fine after a week or so's bed rest. Joe remembered they'd said the same about his mother - and she was dead within three months. All Joe could see now was that his precious wife was very ill and he berated himself for not taking better care of her.

Mabel Russell, a near neighbour, called in at some time during the afternoon. Mabel was a good neighbour, she kept herself to herself most of the time, but often turned up trumps in the case of a crisis. In this instance she took Shirley and Simon home with her and gave them tea, then later brought them home, saw them washed and dressed and tucked into bed without disturbing their father, who scarcely noticed the comings and goings. It was only later that Joe discovered that during the day Shirley had answered the door to Joe Grigson who had called for a bag of sugar which she had given him, and to Emily Sanderson who wanted a packet of tea which Shirley had supplied. She had made notes of both these transactions in her neatest handwriting, which to anyone else was nearly illegible, and had told Joe and Emily to pay her Father when they next came to the shop.

***

"I'll have to go home and collect my clothes," Belinda said.

Martha looked up from her knitting. That Belinda was talking at all was a good sign, it was the first thing she had said all day, and Martha was relieved to note that her friend's words carried the implication that she was finally prepared to leave the brute she was married to. "I'll come with you," Martha said firmly.

"That's not necessary." Belinda looked at Martha with eyes that were vague and unfocussed. "I'll go when he's at work."

"You can't be sure he'll go to work," Martha pointed out. "I'd better be there."

Belinda nodded and sank back into her previous apathetic slump.

"Fancy a cup of tea?" asked Martha, but Belinda shook her head.

"Come on now, Belinda, we must get something down you." Martha was growing increasingly worried about Belinda's lack of appetite. Surely that little baby needed plenty of sustenance?

"I don't want anything, Martha, just leave me alone please." Belinda got up and left the room and Martha heard her feet, which wore a pair of Martha's slippers two sizes too large, shuffle along the hall and into the bathroom.

Martha continued her knitting but when Belinda hadn't returned some ten minutes later, she laid the needles to one side and went out into the hall. From behind the closed bathroom door she heard the sound of sobbing. Wisely, she decided not to interfere, it would be best for Belinda to get the tears out of her system. At least it showed she was facing up to things, and Martha knew that the tears were part of the acceptance and healing process.

Monday morning was dull and the rain that woke Martha as it slammed against the window, continued throughout the day. By afternoon Martha decided they were wasting their time waiting for the rain to stop and she gathered together a suitcase and some shopping bags and persuaded Belinda, who was a little brighter than the weather but not much, that now was the time to collect her bits and pieces. Now the time had come, Belinda didn't seem to have any objection to Martha accompanying her.

Martha was afraid that Harry might have changed the locks, but it didn't seem to have occurred to him and they entered the house without problem. In the bedroom Martha was shocked by the sparsity of Belinda's wardrobe. Certainly she had known that her friend owned few clothes, it was something Belinda had been unable to hide, but the drawer which contained underclothes was practically empty and each garment looked as if it had been washed a thousand times. Martha made a mental note to go shopping during the week and treat Belinda to some pretty new bras, pants and suspender belts; it might go some-way to cheering her up.

Belinda tried to hide the state of her nightwear, but Martha could see that, like the underwear, it was clean but old. She also noted that strips of material hung at odd angles from the garments as Belinda lifted them from the drawer to transfer them to the case and she guessed they had been torn in one or other of Harry's tantrums.

Apart from the clothes and underclothes and two pairs of shoes there was little that Belinda wanted to take with her. A small box of make-up, a couple of hard-back books, a bible - broken at the spine, and a teddy bear. Belinda picked up the teddy bear from its position on the dressing table and held it close to her. "Harry gave me this," she said to nobody in particular, "He won it on the pier, the first time we went out together." She turned and put it in the suitcase. Martha wondered why Belinda would want to keep something that obviously reminded her so much of Harry, but then decided it might be a blessing in the long run. The bear would remind Belinda that she and

Harry had been happy once and that all the years they'd been together had not been completely wasted.

"I was thinking," Martha said as they walked along the street back to Martha's - Belinda apparently unaware of the curious stares from people they passed, "We can turn my sewing room into a nursery."

Belinda's face registered no emotion. No pleasure, Martha noted, no pain, no anticipation.

"Don't you think that's a good idea?" Martha wanted to know.

"Oh, I don't know," said Belinda, with about as much animation in her voice as a stuffed pear. "If you say so, I suppose."

"It's not for me to say, dear," Martha said gently, "We'll wait until you feel up to making a decision, but I think it could be a good plan."

After Belinda had gone to bed worn out with her grief the previous evening, Martha had sat and worked out her financial situation. She thought she would just about to manage to keep herself and Belinda and the baby. If Belinda wanted to go to work after the baby was born, Martha would be able to look after him - she was sure it would be a boy - and that way they would have a little left over for luxuries. Still, they would have to wait and see, Belinda might not want to leave the child, Martha understood that lots of women felt that way, apparently the bond between mother and child was so strong it could scarcely be broken. Martha had never had a child of her own and occasionally she was envious of the closeness she saw between most of the families in the village. Still, she reminded herself that although she might be mother to none, she was certainly 'auntie' to an ever growing tribe of local children - and soon there was to be another member of that happy band. Perhaps, who knew, Belinda's child might look on Martha as something even more than a casual 'auntie'.

***

Nearly every woman in the village visited the store during the following week. Most of them offered help, all of them enquired as to Hannah's well-being. Jenny Elliot and Maureen practically ran the shop single-handed for the first couple of days until Joe began to believe that Hannah was going to get better. Jenny took care of the day-time, although Maureen had managed to recruit various people to help out for the busy periods, and as soon as Scarlett was home, Maureen cycled up to do her stint behind the counter until closing time. Daphne Taylor had proved a brick, had given up most of her days to help out both in the shop and with Simon. When Shirley arrived home from school she and Simon were whisked away to Daphne's home to wait for Leo. The four of them would then sit down to dinner together and then Daphne would take them Shirley and Simon home and put Simon to bed. Shirley was allowed to stay up for a few hours and it was during this time that she amazed her father and later, as she became more conscious of what was going on around her, her mother.

She crept around the house "So as not to wake Simon or Mum," she explained. She made cups of tea and toast for her father with an almost irritating frequency. She was polite and well-behaved, went to bed when Joe remembered to tell her to and was generally nothing like the child she had been up until her mother's illness. That she was worried about her mother was without question, although she seemed to accept the fact that it was a short-term thing and that her mother would soon be back to normal; it was Joe who took longer to reach this belief. Nonetheless, by Wednesday, when the shop closed for the afternoon and Hannah spent several periods of wakefulness in which she sat up and read a magazine, he began to have more confidence in his wife's eventual recovery.

When Daphne arrived at nine o'clock on the Thursday morning, having seen Leo off on the school bus, she made her usual enquiry as to Hannah's state of health. Joe thought for a few moments before deciding that Hannah was probably about ready for some company other than his or the children's. He suggested that Daphne came and sat for a while with Hannah after lunch and Daphne seemed delighted. "I'll have to be back by three thirty to meet Leo's bus. How about if we come back about one?" She indicated Simon, who was to spend the morning with her.

"That will be great," Joe said. I was telling Hannah this morning that I ought to get out and do a few deliveries."

"Of course, I never thought - what's been happening about the orders the past few days?" Daphne knew that some elderly people in the village relied on Joe's weekly delivery to their homes.

"Oh, it's been taken care of," Joe reassured her, "Sam Elliot and Joe Grigson between them have covered all the regular orders, and we haven't taken on anything extra. Still, we can't be taking advantage of people and your being here with Hannah will mean I can get out for an hour without worrying."

"That's good. Right, we'll be off then, all right, Simon? Say goodbye to Daddy."

The shop bell pinged as the door was opened and Ken Barrett stood there. Joe thought at first that he was going to speak to Daphne and Joe remembered that it had been Ken Barrett who had taken Daphne and Nita to the hospital that day. Joe watched as Ken glanced down at Simon, then pushed past the boy and Daphne and walked up to the counter. Daphne looked back at Joe, shrugged, then walked out of the shop.

Without being asked Joe took down the usual packet of cigarettes for his customer. Hannah, undaunted by the man's apparent unfriendliness, had once asked him why he came in every day for a single packet and didn't stock up once a week. Mr. Barrett had told her that coming out for his smokes every day meant that he made sure he got his daily intake of fresh air. He didn't buy much else in the shop and Joe guessed that he did his main shopping in town.

Joe gazed out of the window as his customer fumbled in his pocket for change. Daphne and Simon were strolling along, Daphne looking down at the boy as Simon chatted nineteen to the dozen. It was strange, Joe mused, how everyone had looked upon Daphne as stuck-up and snobbish, with the possible exception of Hannah who managed to see good in everybody. Something had definitely happened to change that woman, he thought, he didn't know how he would have managed without her this week.

"Know someone called Taylor?" asked Ken Barrett suddenly. "Mr. D. Taylor?"

Joe thought for a moment. The only Taylor he knew was Daphne, and she was certainly no Mister. He shook his head. "Sorry, no. Problems?"

"It's this damn business about the car park." Ken Barrett looked at Joe intently. "Not involved in it yourself, are you?"

"Oh, no. No, not me. Have to be seen not to take sides in my line of business, you know." Joe cleared his throat. He thought it prudent not to admit to being wed to the person who had chaired Saturday night's meeting. "So what's happened then?"

"Oh, it's a lot of fuss about nothing really. Trouble is their attitude. After all, it's my land, and only I have the right to decide what the land is used for." He obviously assumed, correctly, that Joe would know all about the situation. Joe guessed he had lived in villages before and was used to the grapevine system that operated in such places. Joe watched as the other man put the cigarettes and change in his pocket and turned to leave. At the door he turned round.

"As a matter of fact, if it had just been the letter I would probably have taken the fence down. After all, if the villagers have been parking there as long as they say they have - a fact I didn't know about when I put the fence up, incidentally, - then they could have continued to park there for all I care. However, it didn't stop at the letter. The fence has been cut in several places, and I've had to suffer abuse that has been hurled at me from people walking down the lane. I don't have to put up with that, Mr. Hughes, and you can tell the people concerned that I said so."

He slammed the door behind on his way out.

"Phew," Joe wiped his forehead as Jenny Elliot came in.

"What have you done to upset our Mr. Barrett?" she joked, "He looked furious."

"I haven't done anything, but I can't say the same for Hannah." He looked up at the ceiling where a loud knocking was coming from. "Sounds like she's awake, she'll have heard the slamming of the door and want to know what's going on. I'd best go and tell her."

"I take it she's getting better."

"Oh, aye, she's coming along." Joe left the shop in Jenny's capable hands and went to bring his wife up to date with developments.

***

It was a few years since Daphne had looked after a two-year-old and she was thoroughly enjoying it. Simon was going on three and quite advanced for his age, she thought, although she had to remind herself that Leo had not been an ordinary child and it would be a mistake to compare other children with him.

She and Simon had already settled into a routine. A drink first, tea for Daphne and milk for

Simon, then half an hour with a book which Daphne would read to him and to which he would listen avidly. It was the only time he was quiet, the remainder of the time he kept up an incessant chatter. Once his attention began to wander from the story they would wrap up warm and go for a tramp across the fields hand in hand. Simon seemed to enjoy it, especially if they spotted any wild animals. On the Tuesday morning they had seen a stoat or a weasel, Daphne had never known which was which, and Simon had jumped up and down excitedly, giggling and gurgling as he did so. When they had got home Daphne had borrowed one of Leo's books and found the picture of the stoat similar to the one they had seen. Simon loved it. "Me see, me see," he laughed as he pointed to the picture.

"That's right, you did, didn't you, Simon? You'll have to tell your Mummy when you get home."

Daphne told Leo of the incident that evening when he got home from school and, in a gesture characteristic of her son, he insisted that Simon be given the book. "He'll be able to look at the pictures," he'd said when Daphne had pointed out that Simon was too young to read. So Daphne had told Simon that the book belonged to him now, although she wasn't sure he fully understood the concept, particularly as she was going to keep the book at hers for the duration of Hannah's illness. Still, Simon did enjoy looking at the pictures and Daphne thought he would probably develop the same interest in wildlife as Leo had.

On the Thursday morning she found she wasn't paying her usual attention to Simon's chatter. Not that it really mattered, he didn't seem to notice. Daphne was thinking how nice it was that Joe had dropped the 'Mrs. Taylor' at last and resorted to 'Daphne'. She had found that Christian names sprung easily to the women of the village, but the men maintained a more formal courtesy of addressing female acquaintances by their full title. That Joe now called her by her first name indicated that he considered her a friend.

She found her thoughts straying to Ken Barrett and his brusqueness in this morning's encounter. At first she had thought he was going to speak, and had she had been unaccountably hurt when he had ignored her totally. Perhaps the locals were right and there wasn't, after all, a soft centre to the rough exterior of the man. She sighed.

"Matter?" Simon asked.

"Nothing, darling. Look, look at that big black bird," She pointed at the rook in the tall tree and Simon's attention was diverted.

***

"So it looks as though there'll have to be another meeting on Saturday night," Maureen said, replacing her hair-brush on the dressing table and turning round on her stool to face Dan who was already in bed.

"I suppose we'll have to go again," said Dan in mock resignation.

Maureen didn't bother to reply as she took off her dressing gown and hung it neatly on the hook, unlike her daughters who both flung theirs on the bedroom floor. She climbed into bed, glad of her husband's warmth in the chilly bedroom.

"I don't suppose Hannah will be there," she said, snuggling up.

Dan put his arm round her and pulled her to him. "How is Hannah today?"

"Oh, she's getting on. Daphne Taylor called in to see her this afternoon. Apparently Doctor Jean told Joe that it would be good for Hannah to have one or two visitors now. Just for a little while. Actually Daphne stayed an hour and Joe said Hannah was tired when she left, but that he thought talking to Daphne had done her the world of good." She sat up slightly and turned to face her husband. "Daphne's been ever so good, you know, she's had Simon all week and Shirley as well after school." She snuggled down again. "I don't know what we're going to do about Ken Barrett, though. I guess someone will have to go and see him."

"Well, it's easy enough to guess who's been cutting the fence, isn't it?"

"Oh?"

"Yes. Young Russell Gibson and that group of lads he goes around with. A pair of wire-cutters and a few snips of wire in the dead of night is right up their street. Given any other circumstances and it would be put down to youthful high-spirits, but, because of Ken Barrett blaming that for the loss of car parking those young urchins are going to find themselves in a spot of bother if they're found out."

"Mmm, you could be right, it certainly is the sort of thing they'd get up to."

"Oh, I'm right, you mark my words. Talking of urchins, when's our little 'un going back to school?"

"I thought she might be well enough to go back tomorrow. I know it's Friday and it hardly seems worth it, but I thought it would break her in gently."

"Good idea." Dan planted a kiss on his wife's dark hair, then moved his lips down to hers as a familiar warmth flowed through him.

CHAPTER SEVENTEEN

Martha thought that she and Belinda had been very lucky, but she found herself wondering how long their luck could last. She had expected Harry to come knocking on the door every day since Sunday, belligerent and violent. She was steeling herself for a confrontation that hadn't happened.

Belinda was gradually getting some colour back to her cheeks although she was still very lethargic. She had seen Doctor Jean twice in the week and the doctor had declared herself satisfied with her patient's progress.

"If you go on looking after her," she had said to Martha, "Belinda will bloom in no time at all. There's no reason why, now she's out of her husband's clutches, that the remainder of her pregnancy should present any problems at all. The baby seems fine and undamaged, and all mother needs is some tender, loving care. See to it." The Doctor had swept out of the house and on to her next call, her brusque manner and often clipped speech hiding a heart that was as soft as putty.

"Well, dear," Martha said to Belinda as she buttered her toast on the Friday morning. " What would you like to do today?" She had asked the same question every day that week, but silence was the only answer she had received - that or a mumbled "nothing".

This morning wasn't going to be any different, Martha thought, as Belinda shook her head and said nothing, until suddenly a light went on in the younger woman's eyes.

"Could we go shopping, do you think?" she asked, then the light went out. "Oh, I haven't got any money." She hung her head, dejection apparent in every nuance of her body.

"Never mind," said Martha, glad because her friend had finally shown a spark of vitality. "I've got a little put away, dear. What was it you wanted to buy?"

Belinda looked up, her eyes sparkling with unshed tears. "I wanted to buy something for the baby," she said, "He's all I've got now."

"You've got me as well, I'll look after you, dear." Martha poured Belinda a fresh cup of tea and passed it across. "Still, you're right, we ought to start getting together a trousseau for the baby. She stood up and walked over to the sideboard, taking from the drawer a bundle wrapped up in tissue paper, which she placed in front of her friend.

"There you are, that's for you - or rather, for your little baby."

"Oh, Martha," Belinda breathed, looking up, "Thank you." She carefully unwrapped the delicately knitted baby clothes. Martha had certainly been busy, everything was there from little tiny vests to matinee jackets to dungarees. "They're beautiful, really beautiful." She fingered the garments as though unable to believe that they were for her and Martha was pleased to see the pleasure she had given. She hugged the younger woman.

"There's still lots of other things the baby will need," she said. "Nappies and things. We'll go into town after breakfast and make a list with prices, then we'll come back here and see what we can afford to buy."

Belinda nodded. "All right, Martha," she said obediently, then a shadow crept across her face, "But I can't keep taking from you, you've done so much already."

"Don't worry about that now, dear, let's just get you strong and well again."

***

Daphne sat and looked at the letter in her hand, unable to believe what she had just read. It was impossible for her to take in the news that her husband was dead.

As usual, she had left the mail to be opened when she got back with Simon who was chattering away in his normal fashion, unaware that he had lost his listener to more important matters.

The letter was from her husband's solicitors. It appeared that Derek had, at least, had the foresight to set up a trust fund, which would give her a regular income so that she and Leo could maintain the standard of life they now had. If Daphne married again, the monthly amount she received would be reduced considerably, but that was a situation Daphne couldn't see arising.

She felt breathless as she began to consider the difference this would make to her life. She supposed to an outsider, viewing her, nothing would seem to have changed, but a feeling of great relief was slowly seeping into her, washing through her veins and into her heart. She felt as though a burden that she had been carrying for so long that it was now no longer noticeable had been lifted. She was free!

With an uncharacteristic whoop of joy, she jumped up, scooped Simon from his chair and swung him round in a gesture of pure abandon. "Come on, my lad, we're off for our walk."

She felt she had to tell someone, and the only person possible was June, who, by nature of her engagement to Des, was one of the few people privy to Daphne's secret.

Their steps took them past the shop, where Joe was taking advantage of an apparent lapse of business by standing in the doorway breathing in the fresh air. It was a lovely bright morning, the air carried on it just a hint of the spring that was waiting round the corner and in the ditches primroses smiled. Walking towards them Daphne saw Ken Barrett, a clutch of envelopes in his hands and the four of them came together outside the shop.

"Daddy," Simon squealed excitedly and Daphne let go of her young charge's hand. He ran to his father who picked him up. "Hello, young fellow, where are you off to, then?"

"Walk," Simon said simply.

Ken Barrett, who had been standing back walked forwards towards Daphne. She immediately sensed a change of attitude in him from that which he had adopted at their previous meeting. "I've been meaning to ask you," he said, "How is the young lady I played 'knight in shining armour' to?"

"What? Oh, you mean Nita. I think she's getting on nicely, isn't she, Joe?"

"Aye, she is. Gone back to school today, I believe." Joe put his son down and Daphne took Simon's hand again.

"Nita's Mum works in the shop," she explained to Ken Barrett.

"Yes, of course." He patted Simon on the head and Daphne thought he was probably not used to children. He looked at Joe, "So this lad is *your* son, is he?"

Joe nodded, proudly. "That's right." He nodded at Mabel who had come out of her house. She said a cheerful good morning to Daphne and Ken as she went into the shop, followed by Joe.

"Funny," said Ken Barrett, "I thought when I saw you earlier that this young man belonged to you, but I can see he doesn't now. He's much too like his Dad to belong to anyone else."

Daphne looked down at Simon. "No, he's not mine. I do have a son, though."

"Oh."

How could one word display so much disapproval, Daphne wondered? She supposed that it was because it was accompanied by a glance at her ring finger, which no longer wore a wedding band.

"Yes," she continued, "He goes to the special school in town. My husband's dead."

Now why on earth had she said that? It must be the relief at being at last able to say it with truth. "Yes," she continued, with a certain pleasure, "It's just me and Leo now."

"I see. You must bring your son round to the Big House one day. Does he like animals?"

"He loves them."   No understatement that, Daphne thought.

He might enjoy a visit, then. I've lots of books and things. I'm a zoologist, you see."

No, Daphne didn't really see.   Couldn't understand why she, or rather Leo, had been given this invitation.   She couldn't understand, either, why her heart was suddenly beating nineteen to the dozen and the world seemed to have shrunk into the dark eyes, which gazed at her.   For a minute she thought ah, zoologist, no wonder he's a bit stuffy. Then suddenly she had known he wasn't stuffy, just a bit shy. Inside that brittle exterior there was a lot of sensitive man, just waiting...for what?

"Auntie Daphne." The tug on her coat sleeve brought her back to the present, to the village street and she felt a blush colour her cheeks. She had been staring at the man. Quite unforgivable behaviour.

"Well?" Ken Barrett appeared to be waiting for an answer and she couldn't remember having heard the question.

"Err...yes," she mumbled, hoping it was the right answer.

"That's good. Maybe at the weekend."

"Err...yes." Now she was repeating herself in an inane fashion and she was still unsure what she was letting herself in for.

"Good. Anytime. You will come with him, won't you?"

Then she remembered, he'd been saying that Leo could go and visit. Daphne gathered her wits about her.

"Yes, of course. That will be lovely. Will Sunday afternoon be all right."

"Perfect." He smiled and Daphne found herself gazing at the way his eyes crinkled when he did so, and little lights that sparkled in his eyes. She thought she saw a touch of amusement there as he nodded, "See you Sunday, then," and continued on his way.

Momentarily disorientated, Daphne allowed herself to be led along by Simon to his favourite spot by the stream that ran along the backs of the gardens in Meadow Lane. She forgot that she had intended to visit June. She watched Simon carefully as he played but a detached part of her mind was thinking all the time of Ken Barrett with his crinkly eyes and of the way she felt when she pictured him. She had never felt like this before, not even about Derek and it was frightening. She had spent a great number of years being in control of her life and now, suddenly, she didn't seem in control any more. Brushing away a stray curl from her forehead, she noticed how hot she was. It felt as though she was running a temperature and she was relieved. There was nothing the matter with her except for the start of a cold. Still, she couldn't help looking forward to the visit to the Big House on Sunday.

***

"So how was school today." Dan was washing his hands at the kitchen sink prior to sitting down to his evening meal. Nita was passing through on her way from the bathroom.

"Okay," she said, stopping and passing the towel to her father. "That new girl's started. You know, the one who lives in the McDonald place. Caroline something-or-other."

Dan tried to remember - Maureen had mentioned the name several times. "Little", he said at last, "Caroline Little."

Nita nodded. "That's right."

"So what's she like, this Caroline?"

Nita put her head on one side and gazed at her father as she thought about the question. "Well, the others don't like her."

"Oh? Why's that, do you think?"

"Well, she's kind of stuck up. As if she thinks she's better than we are. Do you think she could come to tea one day next week?"

The question, coming suddenly after the unflattering appraisal of the new girl, didn't actually surprise Dan. Nita had always had a soft spot for lame ducks and the less-than-popular.

"You'll have to ask your mother about that, lass. You know things to do with the kitchen don't have anything to do with me."

Nita actually knew that it didn't matter what was being decided, her Father's word would always be final if he cared to make known his wishes. Most of the time, though, he was content to let his wife make the arrangements for everyday things and only chimed in occasionally.

"Mum," Nita called now as she turned and left the kitchen. "Can I have a friend to tea next week?"

Maureen looked up from where she was laying the table. "I don't see why not. Who? Shirley?"

"No, not Shirley," Nita looked thoughtful, "Although maybe she'd better come as well, I don't want her to feel left out."

When the Davidsons had first left the village, Nita had seemed to take up with Shirley as a replacement 'best friend' for Sue. Maureen hadn't been too happy about the arrangement. Shirley didn't strike her as being a good influence; she was too disobedient and wilful for Maureen to really take to her. However, during this week of Hannah's illness Shirley had shown another side of her nature and she had been unable to do enough, either for her mother or her father. Maureen had visibly seen the child grow up and, providing the good behaviour continued, was very happy for Nita to have Shirley as a friend, she might learn some useful habits herself.

"So who is it?" Maureen asked. "I know, let me guess - it's the new Little girl."

"She's not that small."

Maureen, passing her daughter, gave her a quick hug. "I know that, you rascal, and you know what I meant."

"So can they?"

"What, come to tea? I don't see why not. Make sure they both ask their Mums though, won't you. And don't forget Mrs. Soames, from Hill House, is coming to tea next Sunday. I thought you'd like to invite Leo as well, seeing as you're both such good friends of hers. Now, I think it's time you washed your hands, I'm just about to bring the dinner through.

***

"I'll get it," Martha struggled up from the chair and looked across to where Belinda opened her eyes having dropped off to sleep.

"What's that?" she asked.

"The door," Martha explained, "Someone knocked at the door." She was beginning to feel her age, these days, and the arthritis in her knees was starting to seriously make itself felt. The exercise of walking around the town that morning didn't seem to have done her much good at all.

They had spent two hours in the town, choosing clothes and writing down prices. Well, Martha had. The lethargy had crept back into Belinda and she had trailed along obediently but had showed very little interest in what was happening.

Whoever was outside started hammering on the door.

"All right, all right, I'm coming," Martha muttered.

She released the door catch and the door flew open. The giant figure of Harry Miles stood there.

"Where is she?" he demanded.

Martha looked at him coldly, at the bloodshot eyes and the spittle that dribbled from his mouth. He swayed slightly as he stood there and her gaze travelled to the bottle in his hand.

"You're drunk," she said disgustedly.

"Never mind that," he said, peering into the darkness of the hall, "Where's my wife?"

He made to step into the hall and Martha stood in front of him.

"You're not coming in here," she said adamantly.

"Wanna bet," he leered. He shoved her out of the way and she fell to the floor, her arm twisting awkwardly beneath her. She watched as he threw open the living room door.

"Where are you, you bitch?"

There was no escape for Belinda, Martha knew. If she wasn't in the living room then she must be in the kitchen, which led off of it. There were no other doors into the kitchen and only small windows. It was only a matter of time until Harry found her. At that moment she heard Belinda cry out, and Harry's roar of rage.

Ignoring the pain that was shooting up her arm Martha ran to the front door. Daphne Taylor was passing and she hurried over at Martha's urgent beckoning.

"Is something wrong?" she asked.

"Yes. Quick. Go and get some men. Harry Miles is in here and I think he's going to kill his wife."

Martha was gratified by the look of horror on Daphne's face as she quickly absorbed the implications and was immediately off and running down the street.

There was a scream from the kitchen and Martha rushed through the house to the source of the sound. In the kitchen Harry had trapped Belinda between the cooker and the sink. She was forced back against the wall and his hands were around her throat. Her huge frightened eyes swivelled towards Martha and Harry turned round to follow his wife's gaze.

"You stupid interfering bitch. This is all your fault," he shouted, taking his hands from his wife's throat, and Martha backed away as he moved towards her. Unable to shift her eyes from the anger that blazed into her like the poker she used to make the fire up with, she backed into the coffee table and lost her balance. Immediately he was on her and she cried out at the excruciating pain in her arm as he lifted her as though she was a rag doll and slung her across the room. She lay, dazed, where she fell, and then felt herself lifted again. Something smashed into her face and her sight became filmed with red, then she felt as though she was flying through the air once more. Vaguely she was aware that her head smacked against something sharp but she was too far gone to really register the fateful blow. Her pain subsided as she slipped into merciful darkness.

The last trace of lethargy left Belinda as the last traces of the love she felt for her husband vanished. She was later to realise what a tragedy it was that it took a murder to make her stop loving him, but there had been so many factors in her life that contributed to her need for him, no one thing could take the blame.

While Harry's attention was on Martha Belinda fumbled in the kitchen drawer until she found what she was looking for; the long handled, long bladed kitchen knife.

She stood with her arms behind her, pressed between her body and the wall as Harry moved across the floor towards her, like a lion with its prey. She knew that the timing of what she was about to do was of the optimum importance. He mustn't know what was about to happen. His eyes were bolts of lightning and the petrified look on her face was genuine, despite her hidden weapon. He moved towards her, muttering curses as he came. She remained silent and focussed. When he was a few steps away she pulled the knife out, lifted it high above her and, holding it with both hands, plunged it deep into his body in the area where she hoped his heart would be. The curses died on his lips and she watched his face, her hands still round the knife handle. He took a moment to register what had happened, then the anger gave way to surprise, then shock. As he fell towards her Belinda darted to one side and stood, shaking but silent, looking down at the wreck that had been her husband.

She was still there when Ken Barrett and Joe arrived a few seconds later.

CHAPTER EIGHTEEN

It took the community months to come to terms with the loss of Martha Skingsley 'A woman who gave of herself unselfishly until the very last,' as the Reverend Watson had said at her eulogy.

After Daphne had commandeered the help of Joe and Ken on that dreadful day, she had remained at Ken Barrett's house at his suggestion, and had telephone for the police and ambulance. Martha had still been breathing when the medical team had arrived but she had slipped quietly away in the ambulance. In the aftermath Belinda had suffered an awful lot of probing questions about the death of her husband, and was due to stand trial for his manslaughter soon. Everyone was confident that it would be an open and shut case and various members of the village community were prepared to give testimony on Belinda's behalf. In fact, thought Daphne as she walked up the lane, Belinda Miles, considering the circumstances surrounding her, was blooming. Her pregnancy had brought a glow to her fair skin, and soft blushes coloured her cheeks. Her eyes were clear and had a new light in them. She and Daphne had spent a good deal of time talking together; Belinda had obviously felt that their circumstances were similar - both women on their own with young children, and

Daphne had gladly given her the benefit of her experience.

Jenny Elliot had let it be known in the village how much she missed her daughter now she had grown up and left home, and how nice she would think it if she had a baby around - just some of the time.

Joe had let it be known that he was looking for some extra help in the shop, so that Hannah could put in less hours - someone young, he thought, who could do with a few extra pennies in their purse.

Altogether, Daphne thought, things were working out quite well. Not that anything was worth poor Martha's dying, though. The village missed Martha dreadfully; the Church had been full to overflowing for the funeral, a day on which the sun had shone and the daffodils in the Churchyard had seemed to burst forth into bloom overnight. It was such a lovely day that the Revd. Thomas had suggested it was God's way of showing how happy he was to have Martha with him, and somehow Daphne felt better about things after that.

Daphne wondered if the other big event that had happened that fateful day would still have occurred if fate had travelled a different road.

Ken had immediately dropped what he had been doing and left for Martha's in a hurry, but not before he had told her to use the telephone to make the necessary calls. "When you've made your telephone calls, make yourself a cup of tea," he had said, "You look as if you could do with it. I'll see you when I get back."

She had been reluctant to follow his orders, for that was how they could be interpreted, but eventually curiosity got the better of her and she set about looking for the kitchen.

The first door she opened was the living room. Definitely a man's room, she thought, as she observed the leather suite and the dark wood bookcases. There was little else in the room - a small coffee table with a decanter atop it stood beside one of the armchairs, and a tower of books sat on a small basket-weave stool. Dark green curtains and carpet gave the room an overall dark feel, only relieved by the splash of colour in the paintings that hung on the walls.

She retreated into the hall, closing the door behind her and crossed to the door opposite. She opened the door and gasped. This was obviously the dining room, but that was only apparent from the obvious sideboard and dining table. In the bay window stood a desk, but every surface in the room was covered with papers, files and books. Large bookcases flanked one wall while more books and paper littered the floor and spilled out of boxes. She remembered that he was a zoologist and guessed that this was where he worked. She backed out of the room hurriedly, feeling like an intruder, and made her way to the remaining door at the end of the hall.

Opening the kitchen door she walked into a light, airy room. The cupboards were painted bright yellow and Daphne wondered if this was his choice or whether the Davidsons had chosen the decor. She rather thought they had, somehow she couldn't see it being Ken Barrett's style. She crossed the room to the kettle and filled it at the sink. Hearing a noise behind her she swung round, startled, to find herself being scrutinised by a pair of eyes that were more yellow than the paint around her.

"Hello, puss." She put the kettle down and crouched down, holding her hand out. "Here, puss-puss."

The cat, a rather war-torn specimen, decided that she might be worth investigating and laboriously stood up and stretched before deigning to cross the large expanse of floor and sniff her hand. Finding she was holding nothing to keep his interest, he meandered off round the kitchen, allowing her only the slightest stroke of his silky fur. It wasn't until the kettle had boiled and she was making the tea that he showed any further interest, and that was because she opened the refrigerator to get the milk. Suddenly he was twining himself round her legs and yelling for attention. She poured some into his bowl and the volume of his purring displayed his gratitude.

Her tea finished, she thought it might be better if she left for home, but her urge to find out what had happened was great enough to prevent her, at least for a while. She passed the time reading the daily newspaper that was open on the table until the sound of car tyres scrunching on the gravel indicated that the owner of the house was home.

She guessed Ken would want a cup of tea himself and she went across to put the kettle on. When he walked in she was pouring the milk into the cups and he told her later that it had seemed so right for her to be there; she looked as if she belonged.

That day seemed so long ago now, she mused, as if it had been in another lifetime. A lifetime before she had known Ken. Really known him, that was.

Arriving at the door to the Big House she knocked at the door. Ken opened it and scooped her into his arms, holding her close.

"I wish you'd use your key," he said as he released her.

She shook her head. "Not until we're married."

"Well, that won't be long, my love."

She smiled, still unable to believe the events that had hurtled her into a relationship as intense as it was sudden, yet with an underlying permanence.

It hadn't been that sudden, of course, it had taken Daphne all of an hour with him that first afternoon to realise that what she had been feeling growing inside her was love; an inexplicable desire to kiss his lopsided grin, a feature that was becoming more and more familiar as she got to know him; and a longing to stroke away the worry lines that seemed to be a semi-permanent fixture on his forehead but which were now less and less prominent.

He, it seemed, had felt the same, although he had waited until their next meeting on the Sunday afternoon to make his feelings felt.

She and Leo had kept their appointment for Sunday tea, and Daphne had taken extra-special care with her appearance. They both left home looking spick and span and she wore the new dress she had treated herself to in a moment of madness. By the time they reached the Big House Leo had already managed to get a smear of dirt down his face and she stood on the doorstep trying to clean it off with her handkerchief. Leo was squirming, "Aw, Mum," he complained as the front door swung open. Embarrassed, and momentarily tongue-tied by the rush of emotion that hazed her vision, Daphne froze on the spot. Ignoring her, perhaps aware of her sudden awkwardness with the sensitivity she was to come to recognise in him, Ken turned his attention to Leo.

"Aha, young Man, I've been looking forward to meeting you."

Leo looked up, surprise on his face. "You have?"

"I have indeed." Ken put his hand on the boy's shoulder and ushered him into the hall, "I think I have some books here that you'd like." He nodded over his shoulder at Daphne, who gathered her wits about her and followed them down the hall and into the dining room. She wondered if he would have cleared up in honour of their visit.

He had. Probably. It was hard to tell, but Daphne thought there were a few less books scattered around the floor, the dining table was actually clear of any object except a huge vase of carnations, obviously brought for the occasion.

Leo wasn't interested in the decor, anyway. With a stunned expression on his face, he was gazing round at all the books. "Cor, look Mum."

"Here you are then, Leo," Ken called the boy over to the desk. I've got some books out especially for you. They're all of animals and I thought you might like to have a look at them."

Obediently, Leo went and sat down, his eyes shining. "I'm just going to make your mother and I a cup of tea, what would you like?"

Leo was already lost in the books.

"A glass of orange squash or milk will do him nicely," Daphne said. "I'll come and give you a hand, shall I?"

"You'll do no such thing," he said sternly. "You're my guest, and guests don't work in this house. However, if you want to come and chat while I get things ready, you'll be very welcome."

So Daphne went out into the kitchen and chatted while he made the tea. They went back into the dining room and she listened while Ken talked to Leo about animals and Leo asked questions and was answered sensibly. So many people spoke to Leo as though he was an idiot and it upset Daphne. Her son wasn't an idiot, he just had learning difficulties; but in some respects his knowledge was above average, and Ken was once again displaying sensitivity in his dealings with Leo.

Later, Leo once again with his head buried in the books, she listened while Ken talked and they whiled away the late afternoon and early evening just relaxing in each other's company and learning more about one another.

Daphne glanced at the clock on the table.

"Good Heavens," she declared, "We must go soon, Leo has school in the morning."

"Just one more cup of coffee?" Ken asked wistfully.

Daphne thought for a moment, then succumbed to the temptation. "Oh, all right then, but it had better be a quick one."

She followed Ken into the kitchen, her feet must have been silent on the carpeted floor, because he didn't seem to realise she was behind him, and when he swung round, apparently to call out to her, she cannoned into him and felt strong arms engulf her. She was never sure whether he had put his arms out to stop her falling or whether it had been a sudden impulse of desire. Either way, the results were the same, a moments eye-contact, then his lips burned down on hers and she gave herself, body and soul, feeling a desire so strong that it took her breath away. He released her suddenly, and she, who had been pressing her body close to his, nearly fell. He turned away, brushing a hand across his face as he did so.

"My God, Daphne, I'm so sorry."

"No, no," she cried, grabbing his arm and turning him back to face her, "Don't be sorry, please."

He hung his head, a look of shame on his face. "But to take advantage of you like that, it was quite unforgivable. Why, I practically forced myself on you."

"There was no forcing," Daphne said quietly and he raised his head and looked into her eyes. What he saw there must have reassured him, for he put out a hand and held hers.

"Since the moment I first saw you I've found myself thinking of little else," he said, "I tried to find out more about you, but it's hard when you don't really know anyone, and you don't want people to know you want to know." He grinned suddenly. "Then I saw you with Joe's little boy and I thought he was yours. I thought you were married and I thought that was it - it was a waste of time. Then you put me out of my misery and I began to hope again. I wasn't even sure what I was hoping for, but now I know." He stood back and, dropping her hand, gave a mock bow.

"Mrs. Taylor, I would be very honoured if you would 'walk out with me'.

She smiled and dropped a curtsey. "Why thank you, kind sir, I would be very pleased to take you up on your kind offer."

He took her hand again. "That's settled then. Well, Mrs. Taylor... hmm, Taylor, Daphne Taylor, D. Taylor..." A frown creased his forehead.

"What is it?" Daphne asked.

"I was just wondering..." he began, but then he shook his head, "No, no it couldn't be, that's too preposterous..."

"Couldn't be what?" Daphne wanted to know.

"Well...you wouldn't happen to have anything to do with this silly business about the parking for the Church would you?"

"Oh." Daphne didn't know what to say and decided to remain silent.

A thunderous look spread across Ken's face as he dropped her hand and stood back. He opened his mouth. Here it comes, she thought, I was so close to happiness and it looks as though that was as near as I'm ever going to get.

"I'm sorry," she said, butting in before he had a chance to say anything. "I only went to the meeting because I thought somebody there had to represent you and I managed to get myself elected to write the letter without even trying." It was her turn to hang her head. "I wish I hadn't done it now. You must think I'm the enemy, here under false pretences."

The strong arms were round her once again. "Of course not! Of course it's not your fault, the villagers were quite entitled to be upset and they were right to get you to write the letter. I was, in fact, going to take down the fence once I learned the facts. But then people started cutting the fences, and making rude remarks when they saw me in the street and I decided not to."

"But now?" Daphne gazed up at him adoringly.

"Well, now that people seem to be accepting me a bit more and instead of moaning about the car park they're congratulating me on being on hand when Martha Skingsley died – not that I did anything, but people seem to think that because I was involved a bit then I must be okay"

Daphne nodded. "They're like that. And, really, you can't blame people for not taking to you at first. You were very brusque."

"I was?"

"You were."

"I didn't mean to be, you know. I just feel uncomfortable around people I don't know." He kissed her lightly on the forehead. "But I'm really glad I've got to know you all now."

"So are you really going to take down the fence?"

"Listen, young lady," he said, putting his finger under her chin and lifting her face to his, "If we're going to spend our lives together you had better learn right now that I never, never, say anything I don't mean. Okay?"

Daphne, who was too busy savouring the words 'rest of our lives' to answer, just continued to gaze at him, but he must have been satisfied, for he put his arm round her. "Right then, coffee coming up."

***

303

It was a beautiful day. The sun beamed down and there was the barest hint of autumn in the air, just enough to stop the day being muggy and overbearing.

Inside the Church it was cool, but not too cool that the ladies of the village couldn't be dressed in their best Sunday summer best. In the front pew Maureen was still running through the list of chores in her head, mentally checking them off one by one and desperately searching for the one she had forgotten. Eventually she decided she had remembered everything and she relaxed, prepared to enjoy the rest of the day.

Across the aisle Eric stood, perspiration standing out on his forehead and nervousness apparent in every nuance of his body.

Behind Maureen Joe held Hannah's hand. She was fully recovered from her illness early in the year, their holiday had put the finishing touches to her recovery and he was determined she was not going to have a relapse of the same trouble.

Belinda was working out well in the shop and her extra help, together with Maureen's, meant that Hannah was doing half the hours she used to do. The extra time she gave Shirley and Simon was paying off dividends, there had been a moment when Joe feared Shirley was going to slip back into her old bad-tempered, disobedient ways, but Hannah had encouraged her to help in the house and Shirley seemed to enjoy it - as long as she could be with Hannah. Left to her own devices she was less than useless, but that didn't matter. She and Hannah did the housework together when Shirley was home from school, then they would take young Simon for a walk before coming home and cooking the dinner. They seemed happy with the arrangement and Joe certainly was. He smiled as he caught his daughter's eye and she smiled back before returning her attention to her brother beside her.

Jenny and Sam Elliot sat halfway towards the back of the Church. Sam was only there under sufferance. "Damn silly affairs, weddings," he'd grumbled.

"Stop grumbling and do try and look cheerful," Jenny had said and now Sam was going about with a silly, insincere smile on his face. Still, thought Jenny, it was a good deal better than the grimace he often wore.

The Jermain family sat in the pew behind Jenny and Sam, eager to see their next door neighbour wedded. David and Jenny Jermain were looking forward to the reception, David because he had heard there was going to be lots to eat and lots of ginger beer, and Jenny because she had heard that Dick Russell was going to be there and she was wearing her first pair of high heeled shoes which she just knew were going to impress him.

At the very back of the Church sat Daphne and Ken. Daphne was thinking of that other sunny day when they had buried Martha. What a tragedy that had been. She had the feeling, though, that Martha would say she hadn't died in vain. After all, she had probably saved Belinda's life.

Daphne gazed at her own new husband and felt the warmth of his love flood round her.

All eyes swivelled to the back of the Church when Peggy Evans struck up the Wedding March on the organ.

His daughters had never looked so lovely, Dan thought, as he walked sedately down the aisle, Scarlett's arm on his. He felt the pride well within him, then he heard Nita snigger and he raised his eyes heavenwards. Still, he had known she wouldn't be able to keep up the good behaviour, he just hoped she managed to get through the service without tripping up or ripping the bridesmaid's dress.

For a while Scarlett had threatened not to have her younger sister attending her.

"She'll spoil it," she'd whined. Well, maybe whined was too harsh a word and, anyway, Dan had to concede that she did have a point, there was a good chance that Nita would do something disastrous before the day was through. He shot a warning glance over his shoulder at Nita and she caught his eye and sobered up. Privately he thought Eric's young sister, who was the other bridesmaid, looked just as likely to get up to mischief as his own younger child. It might prove altogether a disastrous coupling.

The wedding went without a hitch.

Afterwards, Scarlett and her new husband were covered in confetti until the Churchyard was awash with colours of purest pastels.

As they stood, bathed in sunlight, watching the bride and groom have their photographs taken with the bridesmaids, Dan drew his wife to him.

"I love you, Maureen Evans."

Maureen, her eyes still a little red-rimmed from the tears she'd shed at the thought of losing her daughter, smiled shakily, the tears still close at hand.

"I love you, too," she whispered, and clasped his hand in hers, "Never let me go."

"Oh no, I'd never do that." He kissed the tip of her nose gently. "Don't you know you're the loveliest woman here?"

"Oh, you," she giggled in the disarming way she sometimes did as she gave him a playful push. For a few moments it seemed as they were alone, cocooned in the love that hung between them.

"Mum, Dad, come on, we want you in the photos." The moment lost, but only for a while, they took their place in the picture, surrounded by the people they loved.